THE
THREE
MUSKETEERS

* * *

Signet Books proudly presents the exclusive movie edition of Alexandre Dumas' famed adventure novel, once called the world's most widely read book after the Bible.

The romantic French classic has been brought to the screen in several previous versions, notably the Douglas Fairbanks, Sr. movie of silent days, a "talkie" by RKO in the '30's, and a later more fanciful MGM Technicolor adaptation. Producer Alexander Salkind and 20th Century-Fox offered to a delighted worldwide audience the 1974 version, directed in frolicsome, hugely entertaining style by acclaimed director Richard Lester, with a brilliant cast of international stars. In Great Britain it was honored by being chosen the Royal Command Performance Film for 1974.

Signet has specially prepared this edition of THE THREE MUSKETEERS in order that modern-day readers of all ages may thrill anew to the glories of Dumas' greatest romance.

* * *

Other SIGNET Movie Tie-ins You'll Enjoy

The Three Musketeers

By

ALEXANDRE DUMAS

ABRIDGED EDITION

A SIGNET BOOK

NEW AMERICAN LIBRARY

TIMES MIRROR

First published 1844. Special contents of this newly edited
and abridged edition, based on the original English
translation, copyright © 1974 by The New American
Library, Inc.

SIGNET TRADEMARK REG. U.S. PAT. OFF. AND FOREIGN COUNTRIES
REGISTERED TRADEMARK—MARCA REGISTRADA
HECHO EN CHICAGO, U.S.A.

SIGNET, SIGNET CLASSICS, MENTOR, PLUME and
MERIDIAN BOOKS are published by The New American
Library, Inc., 1301 Avenue of the Americas,
New York, New York 10019

FIRST PRINTING, JUNE, 1974

5 6 7 8 9

PRINTED IN THE UNITED STATES OF AMERICA

ALEXANDRE DUMAS
(1802–1870)

The famed French novelist was a large man in person, personality, and achievement. He was the son of a mulatto French Revolutionary general, punished by Napoleon for plain speaking. In life and work, Dumas was influenced by his heroic father, and by the romantics, Byron and Scott. He won fame first for his plays, but he also wrote history, magazine journalism, travel books, and a huge output of romantic "cloak and sword" novels, his complete works eventually totaling 277 volumes. In addition to *The Three Musketeers* and its sequels, *Twenty Years After* and *The Vicomte de Bragelonne*, his most popular works include *The Count of Monte Cristo* and *The Black Tulip*. It is believed several collaborators sketched out material which Dumas rewrote, immortalizing these composite works by his own immense gusto. He earned much money from his writing, but spent lavishly and died in debt.

The Three Musketeers, here published in a special abridged edition for modern readers, is the best-loved of Dumas' books and one of the most celebrated adventure novels of all time. It was once considered the most widely-read book in the world other than the Bible.

The
Three
Musketeers

I

On the first Monday of the month of April, 1625, the town of Meung appeared to be in as perfect a state of revolution as if the Huguenots had just made of it a second La Rochelle, the fortified town where they were now being besieged by the King of France.

In those times, panics were common. There were nobles, who made war against each other; there was the King, Louis XIII, who made war against his great minister, Cardinal Richelieu, not on the field of battle but in the council chamber; there was Spain, which made war against the King, though he had married Anne of Austria, the sister of the King of Spain. And there was the Cardinal, who made secret war against the Queen, a beautiful woman neglected by her husband, so that at this time France lacked an heir to the throne.

It resulted, then, from this habit, that on the said first Monday of the month of April, 1625, the citizens, on hearing the clamour, rushed toward the hostel of The Jolly Miller.

On their arrival the cause of this hubbub was apparent to all.

It was a young man, whose portrait we can sketch in a few lines. Imagine yourself Don Quixote at eighteen; Don Quixote clothed in a woollen doublet. Imagine to yourself, further, a long, brown face, with high cheek bones. Our young man wore a barret-cap, set off with a sort of feather. He had an open and intelligent eye, and a hooked but finely chiselled nose. Too big for a youth, too small for a grown man, an inexperienced eye might have taken him for a farmer's son upon a journey, had it not been for the long sword, which, dangling from a leathern baldrick, hit against the calves of its owner as he walked, and against the rough side of his steed when he was on horseback.

For our young man had a mount which was the observer

1

of all observers. It was a Bearn pony, from twelve to fourteen years old, of a yellow colour, without a hair in its tail.
This pony, though going with its head lower than its knees,
contrived, nevertheless, to traverse eight leagues a day.

D'Artagnan did not in the least conceal from himself the
ridiculous appearance that such a steed gave him, good
horseman as he was. He had sighed deeply, therefore, on accepting the gift of the pony from M. d'Artagnan the elder.

The same day the young man set forth on his journey, furnished with the three paternal presents, which consisted of
fifteen crowns, the horse, and a letter for M. de Tréville,
captain of the Musketeers.

As he alighted from his horse at the gate of The Jolly
Miller, without any one, host, waiter, or hostler, coming to
hold his stirrup or take his horse, D'Artagnan spied, through
an open window on the ground floor, a gentleman, well-made
and of good carriage, talking with two persons who appeared
to listen to him with respect. Then he looked at D'Artagnan
and roared with laughter.

D'Artagnan fixed his haughty eye upon the stranger and
perceived a man of from forty to forty-five years of age,
with black and piercing eyes, a pale complexion, a strongly
marked nose, and a black and well-shaped moustache.

Now, as at the very moment in which D'Artagnan fixed his
eyes upon the gentleman in the violet doublet, that gentleman
made one of his most knowing and profound remarks respecting D'Artagnan's pony, his two auditors laughed even louder
than before.

"I say, sir—tell me what you are laughing at, and we will
laugh together."

The gentleman withdrew his eyes slowly from the nag to
its master.

"I am not speaking to you, sir!"

"But I am speaking to you!" shouted the young man.

The unknown looked at him again with a slight smile, and
retiring from the window, came out of the hostelry with a
slow step, and placed himself before the horse within two
paces of D'Artagnan.

D'Artagnan, seeing him approach, drew his sword a foot
out of the scabbard.

"This horse is decidedly, or rather has been in his youth, a
buttercup," resumed the unknown, continuing the remarks he
had begun, and addressing himself to his friends at the win-

dow, without paying the least attention to the exasperation of D'Artagnan, "It is a colour very well known in botany, but till the present time very rare among horses."

"There are people who laugh at a horse that would not dare to laugh at its master," cried the young D'Artagnan.

"I do not often laugh, sir," replied the unknown, "but I claim, nevertheless, the privilege of laughing when I please."

"And I," cried D'Artagnan, "will allow no man to laugh when it displeases me!"

"Indeed, sir," continued the unknown, more calm than ever,—"Well! that is perfectly right!" and, turning on his heel, he was about to re-enter the hostelry by the front gate.

But D'Artagnan was not of a character to allow a man, who had had the insolence to laugh at him to escape him in this way. He drew his sword entirely from the scabbard and followed him, crying:

"Turn, turn, Master Joker, lest I strike you from behind!"

"Strike me!" said the other, turning sharply round and surveying the young man. "Why, my good fellow, you must be mad!"

He had scarcely finished, when D'Artagnan made such a furious lunge at him, that if he had not sprung nimbly backward, he would have jested for the last time. The unknown, perceiving that the matter had gone beyond a joke, then drew his sword, saluted his adversary, and placed himself on his guard. But at the same moment his two friends, accompanied by the host, fell upon D'Artagnan with sticks, shovels, and tongs. This caused so rapid and complete a diversion to the attack, that D'Artagnan's adversary sheathed his sword, muttering nevertheless:

"A plague upon these Gascons! Put him on his orange horse again and let him begone!"

"Not before I have killed you, poltroon!" cried D'Artagnan, facing his three assailants as well as possible, and never retreating one step before the blows they continued to shower upon him.

The fight was prolonged for some seconds; but at length D'Artagnan's sword was struck from his hand by the blow of a stick and broken in two pieces. At the same moment another blow, full upon his forehead, brought him to the ground, covered with blood and almost fainting.

Fearful of consequences, the host, with the help of his servants, carried the wounded man into the kitchen.

As to the nobleman, he resumed his place at the window.

"Well, how is it with this madman?" he exclaimed, turning round as the opening of the door announced the entrance of the host.

"He is better," said the host; "he has fainted quite away."

"Indeed!" said the gentleman.

"But before he fainted, he collected all his strength to call you, and to defy you while calling you."

"Did he name no one in his passion?"

"Yes! he struck his pocket and said, 'We shall see what M. de Tréville will think of this insult to his protégé."

"M. de Tréville?" said the unknown, becoming attentive. "He put his hand upon his pocket while pronouncing the name of M. de Tréville? Now, my dear host! while your young man was insensible, you did not fail, I am quite sure, to ascertain what that pocket contained. What was there in it?"

"A letter addressed to M. de Tréville, captain of the Musketeers."

"The devil!" he murmured, between his teeth. "Can Tréville have set this Gascon upon me?"

"Host," said he, "could you not contrive to get rid of this frantic boy for me? Where is he?"

"In my wife's room, where they are dressing his hurts, on the first floor."

"Milady must see nothing of this fellow," continued the stranger. "She is already late. I had better go to meet her."

In the meantime, the host found D'Artagnan just recovering his senses. He insisted that he should get up and depart as quickly as possible. Thereupon D'Artagnan half stupefied arose, and, urged forward by the host, began to descend the stairs; but, on arriving in the kitchen, the first thing he saw was his antagonist, talking calmly at the step of a heavy carriage, drawn by two large Norman horses.

A head appeared through the carriage window; a woman of from twenty to two-and-twenty years of age.

Her style of beauty struck him the more forcibly because it was totally different from that of the southern countries in which he had hitherto resided. She was pale and fair, with long, blonde curls falling in profusion over her shoulders; she had large, blue, languishing eyes, rosy lips, and hands of alabaster. She was talking with great animation to the unknown.

"His eminence, then, orders me—" said the lady.

"To return instantly to England, and to inform him immediately should the duke leave London."

"And my other instructions?" asked the fair traveller.

"They are contained in this box, which you will not open until you are on the other side of the Channel."

"Very well; and you, what are you going to do?"

"I? Oh, I shall return to Paris."

"What? Without chastising this insolent boy?" asked the lady.

The unknown was about to reply, but the moment he opened his mouth, D'Artagnan, who had heard all, rushed forward through the open door.

"This insolent boy chastises others," cried he, "and I have good hope that he whom he means to chastise will not escape him as he did before."

"Will not escape him?" replied the unknown, knitting his brow.

"No! before a woman, you would not dare to fly, I presume?"

"Remember," said milady, seeing the unknown lay his hand on his sword, "remember that the least delay may ruin everything."

"True," cried the gentleman; "begone, then, on your part, and I will depart as quickly on mine." And, bowing to the lady, he sprang into his saddle, her coachman at the same time applying the whip vigorously to his horses. The two interlocutors thus started at a full gallop, taking opposite directions.

"Base coward! false - nobleman!" cried D'Artagnan, springing forward. But his wound had rendered him too weak to support such an exertion.

Perforce, D'Artagnan remained the night at the hostelry. On the following morning, at five o'clock, D'Artagnan arose, and, descending to the kitchen without help, asked, among other ingredients, for some oil, wine, and some rosemary. With his mother's receipt in his hand, he composed a balsam with which he anointed his numerous wounds, replacing the bandages himself, and positively refusing the assistance of a doctor. Thanks, no doubt, to the efficacy of the Bohemian balsam, and also, perhaps, to the absence of any doctor, D'Artagnan walked about the same evening, and was almost cured by the morrow.

But when the time came to pay for this rosemary, this oil,

and this wine—the only expenses the master had incurred as the young noble had preserved a strict abstinence, while, on the contrary, the yellow horse, according to the hostler, at least, had eaten three times as much as a horse of its size could reasonably be supposed to have done—D'Artagnan found nothing in his pocket but his little, old, velvet purse with the eleven crowns it contained. As to the letter addressed to M. de Tréville, that had disappeared.

"Where is my letter?" cried D'Artagnan. "In the first place, I warn you that it is for M. de Tréville, and must be found."

This completed the intimidation of the host. After the King and the Cardinal, M. de Tréville was the man whose name was perhaps most frequently repeated by the military, and even by citizens.

"Does the letter contain anything valuable?" asked the host.

"Zounds! it does indeed," cried the Gascon, who reckoned upon this letter for making his way at court; "it contained my fortune!"

"Bills upon Spain?" asked the disturbed host.

"Bills upon his Majesty's private treasury," answered D'Artagnan, who, reckoning upon entering into the King's service in consequence of this recommendation, thought he could make this somewhat hazardous reply without telling a falsehood.

"The devil!" cried the host, at his wit's end.

"But it's of no importance," continued D'Artagnan, with Gascon assurance. "It's of no importance, the money is nothing—that letter is everything."

A ray of light all at once broke upon the mind of the host.

"That letter is not lost!" he cried.

"What?" said D'Artagnan.

"No! it has been stolen from you."

"Stolen! by whom?"

"By the nobleman who was here yesterday. He came down into the kitchen, where your doublet was. He remained there some time alone. I would lay a wager he has stolen it."

"Do you mean," said D'Artagnan, "that you suspect that impertinent gentleman?"

"I tell you I am sure of it," continued the host. "When I informed him that your lordship was the protégé of M. de Tréville, and that you even had a letter for that illustrious gentleman, he appeared to be very much disturbed."

"Then he's the man that has robbed me," replied D'Artagnan. "I will complain to M. de Tréville, and M. de Tréville will complain to the King." He then drew two crowns majestically from his purse, gave them to the host, who accompanied him cap in hand to the gate, and remounted his yellow steed. It bore him without any further accident to the gate of St. Antoine at Paris, where its owner sold it for three crowns which was a very good price, considering that he had ridden it hard from Meung.

Thus D'Artagnan entered Paris on foot, carrying his little packet under his arm, and walked about till he found an apartment to be let on terms suited to the scantiness of his means.

After which, satisfied with the way in which he had conducted himself at Meung, without remorse for the past, confident in the present, and full of hope for the future, he retired to bed and slept the sleep of the brave.

II

M. de Tréville had really commenced life as D'Artagnan now did—that is to say, without a sou in his pocket, but with a fund of courage, shrewdness, and intelligence. He had become the friend of the King, and now he was the leader of that elect band of warriors known as the King's Musketeers.

When Cardinal Richelieu saw the formidable bodyguard with which Louis XIII surrounded himself, he became desirous to have his own guard. The two powerful rivals vied with each other in procuring the most celebrated swordsmen. It was not uncommon for Richelieu and the King to dispute over their evening game of chess upon the merits of their servants, whom they secretly excited to quarrel, deriving satisfaction or regret from the success or defeat of their own combatants.

The day on which D'Artagnan presented himself to M. de Tréville, the assemblage was imposing. When he had once passed a massive door, covered with long square-headed nails, he fell into the midst of a troop of men of the sword, who were calling out, quarrelling, and playing tricks upon each other.

D'Artagnan, however, being a perfect stranger in the crowd of M. de Tréville's courtiers, and this being his first appearance in that place, was at length noticed, and a person came to him and asked him his business there. At this demand he gave his name very modestly, laid stress upon the title of compatriot, and begged the servant who had put the question to him to request a moment's audience of M. de Tréville.

Finally, the door of an inner room opened.

"Monsieur de Tréville awaits M. D'Artagnan," cried a servant.

M. de Tréville was at the moment in rather an ill-humour; nevertheless, he saluted politely the young man, who bowed to the very ground. Stepping toward the antechamber, and making a sign to D'Artagnan with his hand, as if to ask his permission to finish with others before he began with him, he called three times, with a louder voice at each time: "Athos! Porthos! Aramis!"

Two Musketeers who answered to the last two of these three names, immediately quitted the group of which they formed a part, and advanced toward the cabinet.

When M. de Tréville had three or four times paced in silence, and with a frowning brow, the whole length of his cabinet, he cried:

"Do you know what the King said to me, and that no longer ago than yesterday evening—do you know, gentlemen?"

"No," replied the two Musketeers, after a moment's silence—"no, sir, we do not."

"He told me that he should henceforth recruit his Musketeers from among the guards of M. the Cardinal."

The two Musketeers coloured up to the eyes.

"Yes, yes," continued M. de Tréville, "and his Majesty was right, for, upon my honour, it is true that the Musketeers cut but a miserable figure at court. M. the Cardinal related yesterday, with an air of condolence not very pleasing to me, that the day before yesterday those damned Musketeers had made a riot in the Rue Ferou, in a cabaret, and that a party of his guards had been forced to arrest the rioters. You were there—you were! Don't deny it; you were recognised. The

Cardinal named you. And Athos—I don't see Athos! Where is he?"

"Sir," replied Aramis, in a sorrowful tone—"he is ill, very ill."

"Ill—very ill, say you? And what is his malady?"

"It is feared that it is the smallpox, sir," replied Porthos.

"The smallpox! That's a pretty glorious story to tell me, Porthos! Sick of the smallpox at his age! No, no; but wounded without doubt—perhaps killed."

"Well, mon capitaine," said Porthos, "it is true that we were six against six. But we were not captured by fair means, and before we had time to draw our swords two of our party were dead, and Athos, grievously wounded, was very little better. They dragged us away by force. On the way we escaped. As for Athos, they believed him dead, and left him very quietly on the field of battle, not thinking it worth the trouble to carry him away. Now, that's the whole story."

"And I have the honour of assuring you that I killed one of them with his own sword," said Aramis, "for mine was broken at the first parry."

"I did not know that," replied M. de Tréville, in a somewhat softening tone. "M. the Cardinal exaggerated, as I perceive."

"But pray, sir," continued Aramis, seeing his captain somewhat appeased, "do not say that Athos is wounded; he would be in despair if that should come to the ears of the King."

At this instant the tapestry was raised, and a noble but frightfully pale head appeared under the fringe.

"Athos!" cried the two Musketeers.

"Athos!" repeated M. de Tréville.

"You have sent for me, sir," said Athos to the latter, in a feeble but perfectly calm voice—"you have sent for me, as my comrades inform me, and I have hastened to receive your orders. I am here, monsieur; what do you want with me?"

And at these words the Musketeer, irreproachably dressed, entered the cabinet with a tolerably firm step. Moved to the bottom of his heart by this proof of courage, M. de Tréville sprang toward him.

"I was about to say to these gentlemen," added he, "that I forbid my Musketeers to expose their lives needlessly; for brave men are very dear to the King, and the King knows that his Musketeers are the bravest fellows on earth. Your hand, Athos!"

And without waiting for the newcomer's answer to this proof of affection, M. de Tréville seized his right hand and pressed it with all his might, without perceiving that Athos, whatever might be his self-command, allowed a slight murmur of pain to escape him, and, if possible, grew paler than he was before.

Then M. de Tréville made a sign with his hand, and all retired except D'Artagnan, who did not forget that he had an audience.

When all had gone out, and the door was closed, M. de Tréville, on turning round, found himself alone with the young man.

"Pardon me," said he, smiling, "pardon me, my dear compatriot, but I had perfectly forgotten you. I respected your father very much," he said. "What can I do for the son?"

"Monsieur," said D'Artagnan, "on coming hither, it was my intention to request from you the uniform of a Musketeer. But after all that I have seen, I have become aware of the value of such a favour, and tremble lest I should not merit it."

"Well, young man," replied M. de Tréville, "it is, in fact, a favour, but it may not be so far beyond your hopes as you believe. Still, I inform you with regret that no one becomes a Musketeer without the preliminary ordeal of several campaigns, certain brilliant actions, or a service of two years in some regiment of less reputation than ours."

D'Artagnan bowed without replying, feeling his desire to don the Musketeer's uniform vastly increased by the difficulties which he learned preceded its attainment.

"But," continued M. de Tréville, "for the sake of my old companion, your father, I will do something for you, young man, as I have said. I dare say you have not brought too large a stock of money with you?"

D'Artagnan drew himself up with an air that plainly said, "I ask charity of no man."

"Oh! that's all very well, young man," continued M. de Tréville, "I myself came to Paris with four crowns in my purse."

D'Artagnan's carriage became still more imposing.

"You should, I was going to say, husband the means you have, but you should also endeavour to perfect yourself in the exercises becoming a gentleman. I will write a letter to-day to the director of the Royal Academy, and tomorrow he will admit you without any expense to yourself. Do not refuse this little service. You will be taught riding, swordsmanship in all its branches, and dancing; you will make some desirable acquaintances, and from time to time, you can call upon me."

D'Artagnan could not but perceive a little coldness in this reception.

"Alas! sir," said he, "I cannot but perceive how sadly I miss the letter of introduction which my father gave me to present to you."

"I certainly am surprised," replied M. de Tréville, "that you should undertake so long a journey without that necessary introduction."

"I had one, sir, but it was stolen from me."

He then related the adventure of Meung, described the unknown gentleman with the greatest minuteness, and all with a warmth and truthfulness that delighted M. de Tréville.

"This is all very strange," said M. de Tréville, after meditating a minute.

"Tell me, had not this gentleman a slight scar on his cheek?"

"Yes, such a one as would be made by the grazing of a ball."

"Was he not a fine-looking man?"

"Yes."

"Of lofty stature?"

"Yes."

"Of pale complexion and brown hair?"

"Yes, yes, that is he; how is it, sir, that you are acquainted with this man?"

"He was waiting for a woman?" continued Tréville.

"He departed immediately after having conversed for a minute with one."

"You did not gather the subject of their discourse?"

"He gave her a box; told her that that box contained her instructions, and desired her not to open it before she arrived in London."

"Was this woman English?"

"He called her Milady."

"It is he!" murmured Tréville. "I thought he was still at Brussels!"

"Oh! sir, if you know who this man is," cried D'Artagnan, "tell me. I am desirous of avenging myself."

"Beware, young man!" cried Tréville. "If you see him coming on one side of the street, pass by on the other!"

"That thought will not prevent me," replied D'Artagnan.

M. de Tréville pressed D'Artagnan's hand, and said to him:

"You are an honest youth; but, at the present moment, I can only do for you that which I just now offered."

"That is to say, sir," replied D'Artagnan, "that you will wait till I have proved myself worthy."

"But wait a minute," said M. de Tréville, stopping him. "I promised you a letter for the director of the Academy; are you too proud to accept it, young gentleman?"

"No, sir," said D'Artagnan; "and I will answer for it that this one shall not fare like the other."

M. de Tréville, having written the letter, sealed it. But at the very moment that D'Artagnan stretched out his hand to receive it, M. de Tréville was highly astonished to see his protégé make a sudden spring, and rush from the cabinet, crying—"Ah! Sangdieu! he shall not escape me this time!"

"Who? who?" asked M. de Tréville.

"He, my thief!" replied D'Artagnan. "Ah! the traitor!" and he disappeared.

III

D'Artagnan, in a state of fury, was darting towards the stairs when, in his heedless course, he ran head foremost against a Musketeer, who was coming out of one of M. de Tréville's back rooms.

"Excuse me," said D'Artagnan, endeavouring to resume his course, "excuse me, but I am in a hurry."

Scarcely had he descended the first stair, when a hand of iron seized him by the belt and stopped him.

"You are in a hurry," said the Musketeer, as pale as a sheet; "under that pretence, you run against me; you say, 'Excuse me!' and you believe that that is sufficient? Do you fancy that because you have heard M. de Tréville speak to us a little cavalierly today, that other people are to treat us as he speaks to us? Undeceive yourself, my merry companion, you are not M. de Tréville."

"Ma foi!" replied D'Artagnan, recognising Athos, who was going to his own apartment, "I did not do it intentionally. Leave your hold, then, I beg of you and let me go where my business calls me."

"Monsieur," said Athos, letting him go, "you are not polite."

D'Artagnan had already strode down three or four stairs, when Athos's last remark stopped him short.

"Morbleu, monsieur!" said he, "it is not you who can give me a lesson in good manners, I warn you."

"Perhaps!" said Athos.

"Ah! if I were not in such haste," said D'Artagnan.

"Mister gentleman in a hurry, you can find me without running, do you understand?"

"And where, I pray you?"

"Near the Carmes Deschaux."

"At what hour?"

"About noon."

"About noon; that will do, I will be there."

"Endeavour not to make me wait, for at a quarter past twelve I will cut off your ears."

"Good!" cried D'Artagnan, "I will be there ten minutes before twelve."

And he set off running as if the devil possessed him, hoping that he might yet find the unknown.

But at the street gate Porthos was talking with the soldier on guard. Between the two talkers here was just room for a man to pass. D'Artagnan thought it would suffice for him, and he sprang forward like a dart between them. But he had reckoned without the wind. As he was about to pass, the wind blew out Porthos's long cloak, and D'Artagnan rushed straight into the middle of it.

"Vertubleu!" cried Porthos, "the fellow must be mad to run against people in this manner!"

"Excuse me!" said D'Artagnan, reappearing under the shoulder of the giant, "but I am in such haste—I was running after someone, and—"

"And do you always forget your eyes when you happen to

be in a hurry?" asked Porthos. "You stand a chance of getting chastised if you run against Musketeers in this fashion."

"Chastised, monsieur!" said D'Artagnan; "the expression is strong. When would you attempt this?"

"At one o'clock, then, behind the Luxembourg?"

"Very well, at one o'clock, then," replied D'Artagnan.

But neither in the street he had passed through, nor in the next could he see anyone.

He began to reflect upon the events that had passed. It was scarcely eleven o'clock in the morning, and yet this morning had already brought him into disgrace with M. de Tréville, who could not fail to think the manner in which D'Artagnan had left him a little cavalier.

Besides this, he had drawn upon himself two good duels with two men, each capable of killing three D'Artagnans.

"What a hare-brained, stupid fellow I am! That brave and unfortunate Athos was wounded exactly on the shoulder against which I must run headforemost like a ram."

"As to Porthos, that is certainly droll, but I am not the less a giddy fool."

D'Artagnan, walking and soliloquizing, had arrived within a few steps of the Hotel d'Arguillon, and in front of that hotel perceived Aramis chatting gaily with three gentlemen of the King's guards.

D'Artagnan was not so dull as not to perceive that he was not wanted. He was seeking in his mind, then, for the least awkward means of retreat, when he remarked that Aramis had dropped his handkerchief, and, by mistake, no doubt, had placed his foot upon it. He stooped, and, with the most gracious air he could assume, drew the handkerchief from under the foot of the Musketeer, in spite of the latter's efforts to keep it there, and, holding it out to him, said:

"I believe, monsieur, that this is a handkerchief you would be sorry to lose?"

The handkerchief was, in fact, richly embroidered, and had a coronet and arms at one of its corners. Aramis blushed excessively, and snatched, rather than took the handkerchief from D'Artagnan's hand.

"Ah! ah!" cried one of the guards, "will you persist in saying, most discreet Aramis, that you are not on good terms with Madame de Bois-Tracy, when that gracious lady has the kindness to lend you her handkerchief?"

Aramis darted at D'Artagnan one of those looks which inform a man that he has made a mortal enemy.

"Monsieur, you will excuse me, I hope," said D'Artagnan.

"Ah! monsieur," interrupted Aramis, "permit me to observe to you that you have not acted in this affair as a man of good breeding should have done."

"What!" cried D'Artagnan, "you suppose—"

"I suppose, monsieur, that you are not a fool, and that you knew very well that people do not tread upon pocket-handkerchiefs without a reason."

"Monsieur, you are wrong to try to mortify me," said D'Artagnan.

"Oh, oh! you take it up in that way, do you, Master Gascon? At two o'clock I shall have the honour of expecting you at the hotel of M. de Tréville. There I will point out to you the best place and time."

The two young men bowed and separated, Aramis ascending the street which led to the Luxembourg, while D'Artagnan, perceiving that the appointed hour was approaching, took the road to the Carmes-Deschaux.

D'Artagnan was acquainted with nobody in Paris. He went, therefore, to his appointment with Athos without a second.

When D'Artagnan arrived in sight of the bare spot of ground which extended along the base of the monastery, Athos had been waiting about five minutes, and twelve o'clock was striking.

Athos, who still suffered grievously from his wound, was seated on a post and waiting for his adversary with that placid countenance and that noble air which never forsook him.

"Monsieur," said Athos, "I have engaged two of my friends as seconds; but these two friends have not yet come."

"I have no seconds on my part, monsieur," said D'Artagnan, "for, having only arrived yesterday in Paris, I know as yet no one but M. de Tréville, to whom I was recommended by my father."

"You embarrass me," replied Athos, with his grand air. "Ah! how my shoulder quite burns."

"If you would permit me—" said D'Artagnan.

"What, monsieur?"

"I have a miraculous balsam for wounds—"

"Well?"

"Well, I am sure that in less than three days this balsam

would cure you; and at the end of three days, when you would be cured—well, sir, it would still do me a great honour to be your man."

"Well, that is well said," cried Athos, with a gracious nod to D'Artagnan, "and I foresee plainly that, if we don't kill each other, I shall hereafter find much pleasure in your conversation. We will wait for these gentlemen, if you please; I have plenty of time, and it will be more correct. Ah! here is one of them, I think."

In fact, at the end of the Rue Vanguard, the gigantic form of Porthos began to appear.

"What!" cried D'Artagnan, "is your first second M. Porthos?"

"Yes. Is that unpleasant to you?"

"Oh, not at all."

"And here comes the other."

D'Artagnan turned in the direction pointed to by Athos, and preceived Aramis.

"What!" cried he, in an accent of greater astonishment than before, "is your second witness M. Aramis?"

"Doubtless he is. Are you not aware that we are never seen one without the others, and that we are called in the Musketeers and the guards, at court and in the city, Athos, Porthos, and Aramis, or the three inseparables?"

In the meantime Porthos had come up. He waved his hand to Athos, and then, turning toward D'Artagnan, stood quite astonished.

"Ah, ah!" said he, "what does this mean?"

"This is the gentleman I am going to fight with," said Athos.

"Why, it is with him I also am going to fight," said Porthos.

"But not before one o'clock," replied D'Artagnan.

"Well, and I also am going to fight with that gentleman," said Aramis, coming on the ground as he spoke.

"But not until two o'clock," said D'Artagnan, with the same calmness.

"But what are you going to fight about, Athos?" asked Aramis.

"He hurt my shoulder. And you, Porthos?"

"I am going to fight, because I am going to fight," answered Porthos.

"And you, Aramis?" asked Athos.

"Oh, ours is a theological quarrel," replied Aramis, making a sign to D'Artagnan to keep secret the cause of their dispute.

"By Jove! this is a clever fellow," murmured Athos.

"And now you are all assembled, gentlemen," said D'Artagnan, "let us begin."

But scarcely had the two rapiers clicked in meeting, when a company of the guards of his Eminence, commanded by M. de Jussac, turned the angle of the convent.

"The Cardinal's guards!" cried Aramis and Porthos at the same time. "Sheathe swords! gentlemen! sheathe swords!"

But it was too late. The two combatants had been seen in a position which left no doubt of their intentions.

"Gentlemen," said Jussac, "Sheathe, if you please, and follow us."

"Monsieur," said Aramis, "pass on your way, it is the best thing you can do."

This raillery exasperated Jussac.

"We will charge upon you," he said, "if you disobey."

"There are five of them," said Athos, half aloud, "and we are but three; we shall be beaten again, and must die on the spot, for, on my part, I declare I will never appear before the captain again as a conquered man."

Athos, Porthos, and Aramis instantly closed in, and Jussac drew up his soldiers.

"Gentlemen," D'Artagnan said, "allow me to correct your words. It appears to me we are four."

"But you are not one of us," said Porthos.

"That's true," replied D'Artagnan. "I do not wear the uniform, but I am one of you in spirit. My heart is that of a Musketeer."

"Well, then! Athos, Porthos, Aramis, and D'Artagnan, forward!" cried Athos.

The nine combatants rushed upon each other with fury.

Athos fixed upon a certain Cahusac, a favourite of the Cardinal; Porthos had Bicarat, and Aramis found himself opposed to two adversaries. As to D'Artagnan, he sprang toward Jussac himself.

Jussac was, as they expressed it in those days, a fine blade. Nevertheless, it required all his skill to defend himself against an adversary, who, active and energetic, departed every instant from received rules, attacking him on all sides at once, and yet parrying like a man who had the greatest respect for his own skin.

This contest at length exhausted Jussac's patience. Furious at being held in check by him whom he had considered a boy, he grew hot, and began to make mistakes, D'Artagnan redoubled his agility. Jussac, anxious to put an end to this, aimed a terrible thrust at his adversary, but the latter parried it, and, while Jussac was recovering himself, glided like a serpent beneath his blade, and passed his sword through his body. Jussac fell like a dead mass.

D'Artagnan then cast an anxious and rapid glance over the field of battle.

According to the laws of duelling at that period, D'Artagnan was at liberty to help whom he pleased. While he was endeavouring to find out which of his companions stood in greatest need, he caught a glance from Athos. D'Artagnan interpreted it. With a terrible bound, he sprang to the side of Cahusac, crying:

"To me, monsieur! guard, or I will slay you!"

Cahusac turned; it was time, for Athos, whose great courage alone supported him, sank upon his knee.

He cried to D'Artagnan, "Do not kill him, young man, I beg of you; I have an old affair to settle with him, when I am sound again. Disarm him only—make sure of his sword; that's it! that's it! well done! very well done!"

This exclamation was drawn from Athos by seeing Cahusac's sword fly twenty paces from him. D'Artagnan and Cahusac sprang forward at the same instant, the one to recover, the other to obtain the sword, but D'Artagnan, being the more active, reached it first, and placed his foot upon it.

Cahusac immediately ran to that of one of the guards that Aramis had killed, and returned toward D'Artagnan; but on his way he met Athos, who, during this relief which D'Artagnan had procured him, had recovered his breath, and who, for fear that D'Artagnan should kill his enemy, wished to resume the fight.

D'Artagnan perceived that it would be disobliging Athos not to leave him alone, and in a few minutes Cahusac fell, with a sword thrust through his throat.

By now, Aramis had also killed one of his adversaries and things were set well for the Musketeers.

Nevertheless, it was necessary to put an end to the affair. The watch might come up, and take all the combatants, wounded or not, royalists or cardinalists. The Musketeers saluted with their swords, and returned them to their sheaths. D'Artagnan did the same; then, assisted by Bicarat, the only one left standing, he bore Jussac, Cahusac, and that one of Aramis's adversaries who was only wounded under the porch of the convent. They then rang the bell, and, carrying away four swords out of five, took their road, intoxicated with joy toward the hotel of M. de Tréville.

They walked arm in arm, occupying the whole width of the street, and accosting every Musketeer they met, so that in the end it became a triumphal march. D'Artagnan's heart swam in delight as he marched between Athos and Porthos.

IV

This affair made a great noise. M. de Tréville scolded his Musketeers in public, and congratulated them in private, then hastened to the King with the news that the Cardinal's men had met defeat.

"Why, this is a victory!" cried the King, glowing with delight.

"Yes, sire."

"Four men, one of them wounded, and another a youth, say you?"

"Hardly a young man; still, he behaved himself so admirably on this occasion that I will take the liberty of recommending him to your Majesty."

"What is his name?"

"D'Artagnan, sire; he is the son of one of my oldest friends—the son of a man who served under your father of glorious memory, in the partisan war."

"I should like to see this young man, Tréville—I should like to see him; and if anything can be done—well, we will make it our business."

"When will your Majesty deign to receive him?"

"Tomorrow, at midday, Tréville."

"Shall I bring him alone?"

"No; bring me all four together; I wish to thank them all at once. Devoted men are so rare, Tréville, we must recompense devotedness."

"At twelve o'clock, sire, we will be at the Louvre."

"Ah! by the back staircase, Tréville, by the back staircase; it is useless to let the Cardinal know."

"Yes, sire."

Punctually, at the hour of twelve, the four comrades were summoned, via the back staircase, to a private room at the palace.

"Come in, my brave fellows," said the King, "come in."

The Musketeers advanced, bowing, D'Artagnan following closely behind them.

"What the devil!" continued the King, eyeing D'Artagnan. "Why you told me he was a young man! This is a boy, Tréville, a mere boy! Do you mean to say that it was he who bestowed that severe thrust upon Jussac?"

"Truly!"

"At this sort of work many doublets must be slashed and many swords broken. Now Gascons are always poor, are they not?" said the King. "Therefore, take these forty pistoles, my fine young warrior."

At that period the ideas of pride which are in fashion in our days did not prevail. A gentleman received, from hand to hand, money from the King, and was not the least in the world humiliated. D'Artagnan put his forty pistoles into his pocket without any scruple; on the contrary, thanking his Majesty greatly.

"There," said the King, looking at a clock, "Thanks for your devotion, gentlemen."

"Tréville," added the King in a low voice, as the others were retiring, "as you have no room in the Musketeers, and as we have, besides, decided that a novitiate is necessary before entering that corps, place this young man in the company of the guards of M. des Essarts, your brother-in-law."

When D'Artagnan was out of the Louvre, and had consulted his friends upon the use he had best make of the forty pistoles, Athos advised him to order a good repast at the Pomme-de-Pin; Porthos, to engage a lackey.

The repast took place that very day, and the lackey waited at table. The meal had been ordered by Athos, and the lackey, furnished by Porthos, was named Planchet.

Meanwhile, the promises of M. de Tréville began to become realities. One fine morning the King commanded M. le Chevalier des Essarts to admit D'Artagnan as a cadet in his company of guards. D'Artagnan, with a sigh, donned the uniform, which he would have exchanged for that of a Musketeer at the expense of ten years of his existence. But M. de Tréville promised this favour after a novitiate of two years, a novitiate which might, besides, be abridged, if an opportunity should present itself for D'Artagnan to render the King any signal service, or to distinguish himself by some brilliant action.

It was now that D'Artagnan had a visitor who requested his confidence.

D'Artagnan dismissed Planchet, and asked his visitor, a common man, to be seated.

"I have heard speak of M. D'Artagnan as of a very brave young man," said the bourgeois, "and this reputation, which he justly enjoys, has determined me to confide a secret to him."

"Speak, monsieur, speak," said D'Artagnan, who instinctively scented something advantageous.

The visitor made a fresh pause and continued:

"I have a wife who is seamstress to the Queen, monsieur."

"Well, monsieur?" asked D'Artagnan.

"Well!" resumed the bourgeois, "my wife was carried off, yesterday morning, as she was coming out of her workroom."

"And by whom was your wife carried off?"

"A man who has pursued her a long time."

"The devil!"

"You appear to be an honest young man, and I will place confidence in you. I believe, then, that love has nothing to do with the carrying off of my wife, as regards herself, but that it has been done on account of the amours of a much greater lady than she is."

"Ah! ah! can it be on account of the amours of Madame de Bois-Tracy?" said D'Artagnan, wishing to have the air, in the eyes of the bourgeois, of being fully acquainted with the affairs of the court.

"Higher, monsieur, higher."

"Of Madame d'Aiguillon?"

"Still higher."

"Of Madame de Chevreuse?"

"Higher, much higher!"

"Of the—?" D'Artagnan stopped.

"Yes, monsieur," replied the terrified bourgeois, in a tone so low that he was scarcely audible.

"And with whom?"

"With whom can it be, if not with the Duke of—"

"The Duke of—"

"Yes, monsieur," replied the bourgeois, giving a still lower intonation to his voice.

D'Artagnan reflected upon this information. He knew the Duke of Buckingham was at this time the greatest man in Britain, with the same relation to King Charles I as that of Richelieu to Louis XIII. He was the King's first minister, and as such devoted much attention to the Royal Navy; unlike Richelieu, he enjoyed the personal friendship of his sovereign, and had represented him at the Court of France. There, the handsomest man in Europe, courtly in breeding and well-versed in gallantry, he had been presented to Anne of Austria.

The marriage of Anne to the King of France had been solely an affair of state. Louis XIII, the late-born son of the greatest and best of kings, Henri IV, after his father's assassination had passed the impressionable period of youth struggling against the domination of his mother, the Queen-Regent Marie de Medici, and her lover Concini. This had given him a dislike of women—so much so that the neglected Queen Anne responded to the passion of the magnificent Duke as tinder to fire. These sentiments, suspected by the King, were known to Cardinal Richelieu, and indeed to others.

"But how do you know all this?"

"I know it from my wife, monsieur—from my wife herself."

"Ah! ah! the plot begins to develop," said D'Artagnan.

"Well, my wife came and confided to me that the Queen at that very moment entertained great fears."

"Indeed!"

"Yes, M. the Cardinal, it appears, pursues her and persecutes her more than ever."

"Indeed!"

"And the Queen believes—"

"Well, what does the Queen believe?"

"She believes that someone has written to the Duke of Buckingham in her name."

"The devil! But what has your wife to do with all this?"

"Her devotion to the Queen is known, and they wish either to remove her from her mistress, or intimidate her."

"That is all very probable," said D'Artagnan; "but the man who has carried her off—do you know him?"

"Oh! certainly; he is a noble of very lofty carriage, black hair, swarthy complexion, piercing eye, white teeth, and a scar on his temple."

"A scar on his temple," cried D'Artagnan; "and with that, white teeth, a piercing eye, dark complexion, black hair, and haughty carriage; why, that's my man of Meung."

"He is your man, do you say?"

"Yes, yes; but that has nothing to do with it. No, I am mistaken; it simplifies the matter greatly. To be sure, if your man is mine, with one blow I shall obtain two revenges, that's all; but where is this man to be found?"

"I cannot tell you."

"Have you no information respecting his dwelling?"

"None; one day, as I was taking my wife back to the Louvre, he was coming out as she was going in, and she pointed him out to me."

"Your name is Bonacieux?" interrupted D'Artagnan.

"Yes, that is my name."

"It appears to me that that name is familiar to me."

"Very possibly, monsieur. I am your landlord."

"Ah, ah!" said D'Artagnan, half rising and bowing.

"And it is three months since you arrived. Engaged as you must be in your important occupations, you have forgotten to pay me my rent; and, as I have not tormented you a single instant, I thought you would appreciate my delicacy."

"How can it be otherwise, my dear Bonacieux?" replied D'Artagnan; "trust me, I am fully grateful for such conduct, and if, as I told you, I can be of any service to you—"

"I believe you, monsieur. I have confidence in you."

"Finish, then, what you were about to say."

The bourgeois took a paper from his pocket, and presented it to D'Artagnan.

"A letter?" said the young man.

"Which I received this morning."

" 'Do not seek for your wife,' " read D'Artagnan; " 'she will be restored to you when she is no longer needed. If you make a single step to find her you are lost.' "

"That's pretty positive," continued D'Artagnan; "but, after all, it is only a threat."

"Yes, but that threat terrified me. Seeing you constantly surrounded by Musketeers of a very superb appearance, and knowing that these Musketeers belonged to M. de Tréville, and are consequently enemies of the Cardinal, I thought that you and your friends, while rendering justice to our poor Queen, would not be displeased at having an opportunity of doing his eminence an ill-turn."

"No doubt."

"And then I thought that, owing me three months' rent, which I have said nothing about—"

"Yes, yes; you have already given me that reason, and I find it excellent."

"Reckoning still further, that as long as you do me the honour to remain in my house, that I shall never name to you your future rent."

"Very kind!"

"And in addition to this, if there be need of it, I mean to offer you fifty pistoles, should you, against all probability, be short at the present moment."

"Monsieur, you have quite won me over," said D'Artagnan. "I offer you not only my services, but those of my three stalwart companions. You may rest assured."

Upon the departure of M. Bonacieux, Athos and Porthos arrived and were quickly followed by Aramis. D'Artagnan related to his friends all that had passed between him and his host, and how the man who had abducted the wife of his landlord was the same with whom he had had the difference at The Jolly Miller in Meung.

"Gentlemen," he said, "let us seek Bonacieux' wife—she is the key to this intrigue."

At this moment Bonacieux rushed back into the room.

"Save me, gentlemen!" cried he. "Four men have come to arrest me!"

Four of the Cardinal's Guards appeared at the door.

"Come in, gentlemen," called D'Artagnan. "We are all faithful servants of the King and the Cardinal."

"Then, gentlemen, you will not oppose our executing the orders we have received?"

"But you promised me—" whispered poor Bonacieux.

"We can only rescue you by being free ourselves," replied D'Artagnan in a rapid, low tone. "Come, gentlemen, remove the fellow," he said while pushing him among the Guards, who were full of thanks as they took away their prey.

"What villainy you have performed!" cried Porthos. "Shame, shame for four Musketeers to allow an unfortunate fellow who cried for help to be arrested in their midst!"

"Porthos," said Aramis, "Athos has already told you that you are a simpleton, and I agree. D'Artagnan, you are a great man."

"And now, gentlemen"—said D'Artagnan, without stopping to explain himself to Porthos—" 'All for one, one for all' is our motto, is it not?"

"And yet—" said Porthos.

"Hold out your hand and swear!" cried Athos and Aramis at once.

Then the four friends repeated with one voice the formula dictated by D'Artagnan:

"All for one, one for all!"

"That's well!" said D'Artagnan. "From this moment we are at war with the Cardinal."

V

The invention of the mouse-trap does not date from our days; as soon as societies, in organizing themselves, invented any kind of police, that police, in its turn, invented mouse-traps.

The apartment of Master Bonacieux became a mouse-trap, and whoever appeared there was taken and interrogated by the Cardinal's people. It must be observed that, as a private passage led to the first floor in which D'Artagnan lodged, those who called to see him were exempted from this.

As to D'Artagnan, he converted his room into an observatory. From his windows he saw all; then having removed some of the boarding of his floor, and nothing remaining but a simple ceiling between him and the room beneath, he heard all that passed between the inquisitors and the accused.

On the evening of the day after the arrest of poor Bonacieux, a knocking was heard at the street-door, which was instantly opened and shut.

D'Artagnan flew to his hole, and laid himself down on the floor at full length to listen.

Cries were soon heard, and then moans, which someone appeared to be endeavouring to stifle.

"The devil!" said D'Artagnan to himself, "it's a woman—they are searching her—she resists—they use force—the scoundrels!"

"But I tell you that I am mistress of the house, gentlemen! I tell you I am Madame Bonacieux—I tell you I belong to the Queen!" said the unfortunate woman.

"Madame Bonacieux!" murmured d'Artagnan, "can I have been so lucky as to have found what everybody is seeking for?"

"Pardon, gentlemen, par—" murmured the voice, which could now only be heard in inarticulate sounds.

"They are binding her, they are going to drag her away," cried D'Artagnan to himself, springing up from the floor. "My sword! good, it is by my side. Planchet!"

"Monsieur!"

"Run and seek Athos, Porthos, and Aramis. One of the three will certainly be at home, perhaps all three are. Tell them to arm, to come here, and be quick!"

"But where are you going, monsieur, where are you going?"

"I am going down by the window, in order to be there the sooner," cried D'Artagnan. "On your part, put back the boards, sweep the floor, go out at the door, and run where I bid you."

"Oh! monsieur! monsieur! you will kill yourself," cried Planchet.

"Hold your tongue, you stupid fellow," said D'Artagnan, and, laying hold of the window-frame, he let himself gently down.

He then went straight to the door and knocked, murmuring: "I will go myself and be caught in the mouse-trap, but woe be to the cats that shall pounce upon such a mouse!"

The knocker had scarcely sounded when the door was opened, and D'Artagnan, sword in hand, rushed into the apartment of Master Bonacieux.

D'Artagnan was conqueror without much trouble. Two or three scratches made by the Gascon's blade had sufficed for their defeat, and D'Artagnan remained master of the field of battle, as four men fled the mouse-trap.

On being left alone with Madame Bonacieux, D'Artagnan turned towards her. The poor woman reclined where she had been left, in a half-fainting state.

She was a charming woman about twenty-five years of age, with dark hair, blue eyes, and a nose slightly turned up, admirable teeth, and a complexion marbled with rose and opal.

"Ah! monsieur!" she said, "you have saved me. Permit me to thank you."

"Madame," said D'Artagnan, "I have only done what every gentleman would have done in my place—you owe me no thanks."

"Oh! yes, monsieur, oh! yes, and I hope to prove to you that you have not served an ingrate. But what could these men, whom I at first took for robbers, want with me, and why is M. Bonacieux not here?"

"Madame, those men were much more dangerous than any robbers could have been for they are the agents of M. the Cardinal; and as to your husband, M. Bonacieux, he is not here, because he was yesterday evening taken away to the Bastille."

"My husband in the Bastille!" cried Madame Bonacieux. "Oh! good God! what can he have done? Poor dear man! he is innocence itself!"

"What has he done, Madame?" said D'Artagnan. "I believe that his only crime is to have at the same time the good fortune and the misfortune to be your husband."

"But, monsieur, you know then—"

"I know that you have been carried off, madame."

"And by whom? Do you know? If you know, tell me!"

"By a man of from forty to forty-five years of age, with black hair, a dark complexion, and a scar on his left temple."

"That is he, that is he; but his name?"

"Ah! his name? I do not know that."

"And did my husband know I had been carried off?"

"He was informed of it by a letter written to him by the ravisher himself."

"And does he suspect," said Madame Bonacieux, with some embarrassment, "the cause of this event?"

"He attributed it, I believe, to a political cause."

"I suspected so myself at first, and now I think entirely as he does. My dear M. Bonacieux has not then for an instant suspected me?"

"Far from it, madame, he was too proud of your modesty, and particularly of your love."

A smile stole almost imperceptibly over the rosy lips of the pretty young woman.

"But," continued D'Artagnan, "how did you escape?"

"I took advantage of a moment at which they left me alone; and with the help of the sheets I let myself down from the window."

"We must leave this house," said D'Artagnan. "We will visit my friend, Athos, if he is at his apartment."

As D'Artagnan had foreseen, Athos was not at home; he took the key, which was customarily given him as one of the family, ascended the stairs, and introduced Madame Bonacieux into the little apartment.

"Here, make yourself at home," said he; "wait here, fasten the door within, and open it to nobody unless you hear three taps like these," and he tapped thrice: "two taps close together and pretty hard, the other at a considerable distance and more light."

"That is right," said Madame Bonacieux. "Now in my turn, let me give you my orders."

"I am all attention."

"Present yourself at the wicket of the Louvre, on the side of the Rue de l'Echelle, and ask for Germain."

"Well, and then?"

"He will ask you what you want, and you will answer by these two words: Tours and Bruxelles. He will immediately be at your command."

"And what shall I order him to do?"

"To go and fetch M. Laporte, the Queen's valet de chambre."

"And when he shall have informed him, and M. Laporte has come?"

"You will send him to me."

"That is all very well; but where and how shall I see you again?"

"Do you wish much—to see me again?"

"Certainly I do."

"Well, let that care be mine."

"I depend upon your word."

"You may."

D'Artagnan bowed to Madame Bonacieux, darting at her the most loving glance that he could possibly concentrate upon her charming little person; and while he descended the stairs, he heard the door closed and double-locked.

Everything went well. Germain brought Laporte to the lodge; in two words D'Artagnan informed him where Madame Bonacieux was.

"Young man," said he to D'Artagnan, "I have a piece of advice to give you."

"What is it?"

"You may get into trouble by what has taken place."

"Do you think so?"

"Yes. Have you any friend whose clock is too slow?"

"What then?"

"Go and call upon him, in order that he may give evidence of your having been with him at half past nine. In a court of justice that is called an alibi."

D'Artagnan found this advice prudent. He took to his heels, and was soon at M. de Tréville's, but, instead of passing to the salon with the rest of the world, he asked to be shown into M. de Tréville's closet. As D'Artagnan so constantly frequented the hotel, no difficulty was made in complying with his request, and a servant went to inform M. de Tréville that his young compatriot, having something important to communicate, solicited a private audience. Five minutes after, M. de Tréville was asking D'Artagnan what he could do to serve him, and what caused his visit at so late an hour.

"Pardon me, monsieur," said D'Artagnan, who had profited by the moment he had been left alone to put back M. de Tréville's clock three quarters of an hour, "but I thought, as it was yet only twenty minutes past nine, it was not too late to wait upon you."

"Twenty minutes past nine!" cried M. de Tréville, looking at the clock; "why, that's impossible!"

"Look, rather, monsieur," said D'Artagnan, "the clock shows it."

"That's true," said M. de Tréville; "I should have thought it was much later. But what can I do for you?"

Then D'Artagnan told M. de Tréville a long history about the Queen. He expressed to him the fears he entertained with respect to her Majesty, and related to him what he had heard of the projects of the cardinal with regard to Buckingham.

As ten o'clock was striking, D'Artagnan left M. de Tréville, who thanked him for his information, recommended him to have the service of the King and Queen always at heart, and returned to the salon. But at the foot of the stairs, D'Artagnan remembered that he had forgotten his cane. He consequently ran upstairs again, re-entered the closet, with a turn of his finger set the clock right again, that it might not be perceived the next day that it had been put wrong, and, certain from that time that he had a witness to prove his alibi, he ran downstairs and soon gained the street.

His visit to M. de Tréville being paid, D'Artagnan pensively took the longest way homeward.

"Poor Athos!" said he, "he will never guess what all this means. How will it all end?"

"Badly! monsieur—badly!" replied a voice, which the young man recognized as that of Planchet.

"How badly? What do you mean by that, you stupid fellow?" asked D'Artagnan; "what has happened?"

"In the first place, M. Athos is arrested."

"What for?"

"He was found in your lodging—they took him for you."

"And by whom was he arrested?"

"By the guards whom the men you put to flight fetched."

"Why did he not tell them his name?"

"He took care not to do so, monsieur; on the contrary, he came up to me and said, 'It is your master that wants his liberty at this moment, and not I, since, he knows everything, and I know nothing. They will believe he is arrested, and that will give him time; in three days I will tell them who I am, they cannot fail to set me at liberty again.'"

"Bravo, Athos! noble heart!" murmured D'Artagnan.

And with all the swiftness of his legs, D'Artagnan directed his course toward M. de Tréville's.

M. de Tréville was not at his hotel. His company was on guard at the Louvre, and he was there with his men.

He must get at M. de Tréville, for it was of importance that the latter should be informed of what was going on. D'Artagnan resolved to endeavour to get into the Louvre. His costume of a guard in the company of M. des Essarts would, he thought, be a passport for him.

As he gained the top of the Rue Guénegaud, he saw two persons coming out of the Rue Dauphine, whose appearance very much struck him. One was a man, the other a woman—the latter very much like Madame Bonacieux in height and step.

The young man and woman perceived that they were watched, and redoubled their speed. D'Artagnan determined upon his course; he passed them, then returned, so as to meet them exactly before the Samaritaine, which was illuminated by a lamp.

D'Artagnan stopped before them.

"What do you want, monsieur?" asked the stranger drawing back a step, and with a foreign accent.

"It is not with you I have anything to do; it is with madame, here."

"With madame! You do not know her!" replied the stranger.

"You are deceived, monsieur; I know her very well."

"Ah," said Madame Bonacieux, in a tone of reproach, "ah, monsieur, I had the promise of a soldier and the word of a nobleman; I thought I might have depended upon them!"

"And I, madame!" said D'Artagnan, embarrassed—"you promised me—"

"Take my arm, madame," said the stranger, "and let us proceed on our way."

D'Artagnan, however, cast down, by all that had happened so strangely to him, still stood with his arms crossed.

The stranger advanced two steps, and pushed D'Artagnan aside with his hand.

D'Artagnan made a spring backward, and drew his sword.

At the same time, and with the rapidity of lightning, the unknown drew his.

"In the name of Heaven, milord!" cried Madame Bonacieux, throwing herself between the combatants, and seizing the swords with her hands.

"Milord!" cried D'Artagnan, enlightened by a sudden idea, "milord! Pardon me, monsieur, but are you not—"

"Milord, the Duke of Buckingham," said Madame Bonacieux in an undertone; "and now you may ruin us all."

"Milord!—madame! I ask a hundred pardons!—but I love her, milord, and was jealous; you know what it is to love, milord. Pardon me, and then tell me how I can risk my life to serve your Grace."

"You are a brave young man," said Buckingham, holding out his hand to D'Artagnan, who pressed it respectfully. "You offer me your services; with the same frankness I accept them. Follow us, at a distance of twenty paces, to the Louvre, and if anyone watches us, kill him!"

D'Artagnan placed his naked sword under his arm, allowed the duke and Madame Bonacieux to proceed twenty steps, and then followed them, ready to execute the instructions of the noble and elegant minister of Charles I.

But fortunately he had no opportunity to give the duke this proof of his devotion, and the young woman and the handsome Musketeer entered the Louvre by the wicket of the Echelle, without meeting with any interruption.

VI

Meanwhile, we must not lose sight of M. Bonacieux.

The mercer was attended by two guards, who made him traverse a court, opened a door and pushed him unceremoniously into an apartment, the whole furniture of which consisted of one table, one chair and a commissary.

This commissary was a man of very repulsive mien, with a pointed nose, yellow and salient cheek-bones, and small but keen, penetrating eyes.

He began by asking M. Bonacieux his name, age, condition, and abode.

The accused replied that his name was Jacques Michel Bonacieux, that he was fifty-one years old, was a retired mercer, and lived at No. 14, Rue des Fossoyeurs.

"Monsieur Bonacieux," said the commissary, looking at the accused, as if his little eyes had the faculty of reading the hidden recesses of the heart, "Monsieur Bonacieux, you have a wife?"

"Yes, monsieur," replied the mercer, in a tremble, "that is to say, I had one."

"What?? you had one! what have you done with her, then, if you have her no longer?"

"She has been carried off from me, monsieur."

"And do you know who the man is that has committed this outrage?"

"I suspect," said he, "a tall, dark man of lofty carriage, who has the air of a great lord."

The commissary appeared to experience a little uneasiness.

"This is a matter for M. the Cardinal, himself," he muttered.

And so it was that Bonacieux found himself taken from the Bastille by closed carriage to a certain discreet doorway off the Rue des Bons Enfants.

The door opened, two guards received Bonacieux. They carried him along an alley, up a flight of stairs, and entered the chamber, where he appeared to be expected.

Standing before the chimney, was a man of middle height, of a haughty, proud mien; with piercing eyes, a large brow, and a thin face, which was made still longer by a royal (or imperial, as it is now called), surmounted by a pair of moustaches.

This man was Armand Jean Duplessis, Cardinal de Richelieu, already weak of body, but sustained by that moral power which made him one of the most extraordinary men that ever existed.

"Is this that Bonacieux?" asked he, after a moment of silence.

"Yes, monseigneur."

"That's well. Give me those papers, and leave us."

"You are accused of high treason," said the Cardinal, slowly. "You have conspired with your wife, with Madame de Chevreuse, and with milord Duke of Buckingham."

"My wife said that the Cardinal de Richelieu had drawn the Duke of Buckingham to Paris to ruin him and to ruin the Queen."

"She said that?" cried the Cardinal, with violence.

"That's exactly what my wife said, monseigneur."

"Do you know who carried off your wife?"

"No, monseigneur."

"We shall know, be assured; nothing is concealed from the Cardinal; the Cardinal knows everything."

At these words he took up a silver bell, and rang it; an officer entered.

"Go," said he, in a subdued voice, "and find Rochefort; tell him to come to me immediately, if he has returned."

"The count is here," said the officer, "and requires to speak with your eminence instantly."

"Let him come in, then; let him come in, then!" said the Cardinal eagerly.

Five seconds had scarcely elapsed after the disappearance of the officer, when the door opened, and a new personage entered.

"It is he!" cried Bonacieux.

"He! what he?" asked the Cardinal.

"The man that took away my wife!"

The Cardinal rang a second time. The officer reappeared.

"Place this man in the care of his guards again, and let him wait till I send for him."

The officer took Bonacieux by the arm, and led him into the antechamber, where he found his two guards.

The newly-introduced personage followed Bonacieux impatiently with his eyes till he was gone out, and the moment the door closed, he advanced eagerly towards the Cardinal and said:

"They have seen each other!"

"The Queen and the Duke?" cried Richelieu.

"Yes."

"Where?"

"At the Louvre."

"How did it take place?"

"At half-past twelve, the Queen was with her women, when someone came and brought her a handkerchief from her dame de lingerie."

"And then!"

"She rose, and with a trembling voice; 'Ladies,' said she, 'wait for me ten minutes, I shall soon return.' She then opened the door of her alcove, and went out."

"Did none of her women accompany her?"

"Only Donna Estefana."

"Did she afterwards return?"

"Yes; but to take a little rosewood casket, with her cipher upon it; and went out again immediately."

"And when she finally returned, did she bring that casket with her?"

"No."

"What was in that casket?"

"The diamond studs which his Majesty gave the Queen."

"Madame de Lannoy is of opinion that she gave them to Buckingham?"

"She is sure of it."

"How can she be so?"

"In the course of the day, Madame de Lannoy, in her quality of tire-woman of the Queen, looked for this casket, appeared uneasy at not finding it, and at length asked the Queen if she knew anything about it."

"And the Queen?"

"The Queen became exceedingly red, and replied that having on the preceding evening broken one of those studs, she had sent it to her goldsmith to be repaired."

"He must be called upon, and so ascertain if the thing be true or not."

"I have just been with him."

"And the goldsmith says?—"

"The goldsmith has heard of nothing of the kind."

"Right! right! Rochefort, all is not lost! and perhaps—perhaps—everything is for the best!"

"What are your eminence's orders?"

"Tell Vitray to come to me," said he, "and tell him to get ready for a journey."

The instant after, the man he required was before him, booted and spurred.

"Vitray," said he, "you will go, with all speed, to London. You must not stop an instant on the way. You will deliver this letter to milady. Here is an order for two hundred pistoles."

The messenger, without replying a single word, bowed, took the letter, with the order for the two hundred pistoles, and retired.

These were the contents of the letter:

Milady—

Be at the first ball at which the Duke of Buckingham shall be present. He will wear on his doublet twelve diamond studs; get as near to him as you can, and cut off two of them.

As soon as these studs shall be in your possession, inform me."

VII

Louis XIII and his Cardinal were closeted together. Scarcely had the last of the attendants closed the door after him that his eminence said to the King:

"Sire, Monsieur de Buckingham has been in Paris five days, and only left it this morning."

"M. de Buckingham in Paris! And what does he come to do there?"

"To conspire, no doubt, with your enemies the Huguenots and the Spaniards."

"No, pardieu! no! To conspire against my honour, with Madame de Chevreuse, Madame de Longueville, and the Condés."

"Oh! sire, what an idea! The Queen loves your majesty too well."

"Woman is weak, monsieur le cardinal," said the King; "and as to loving me much, I have my own opinion respecting that love."

"I not the less maintain," said the Cardinal, "that the Duke of Buckingham came to Paris for a project purely political."

"And I am sure that he came for quite another purpose, monsieur le cardinal."

"Indeed," said the Cardinal, "whatever repugnance I may have to directing my mind to such a treason, your majesty compels me to think of it. Madame de Lannoy, whom, according to your majesty's command, I have frequently interrogated, told me this morning, that the night before last her majesty sat up very late, that this morning she wept much, and that she was writing all day."

"That's it!" cried the King. "Monsieur le cardinal you have heard me; I will have those letters."

"There is but one means."

"What is that?"

"That would be to charge M. de Séguier, the keeper of the seals, with this mission."

"Let him be sent for instantly."

"Your majesty's orders shall be executed; but—"

"But what?"

"But the Queen will perhaps refuse to obey."

"What, my orders?"

"Yes, if she is ignorant that these orders come from the King."

"Well, that she may have no doubt on that head, I will go and inform her myself."

And Louis XIII, opening the door of communication, passed into the corridor which led to the apartments of Anne of Austria.

The Queen was in the midst of her women. Madame Guéméné was reading aloud, and everybody was listening to her with attention, with the exception of the Queen, who had, on the contrary, desired this reading in order that she might be able, whilst feigning to listen, to pursue the thread of her own thoughts.

It was at the moment she was plunged in the deepest of reflections, that the door of the chamber opened, and the King entered.

"Madame," said he, "you are about to receive a visit from the chancellor, who will communicate certain matters to you, with which I have charged him."

The unfortunate Queen, who was constantly threatened with divorce, exile, and trial even, turned pale under her rouge, and could not refrain from saying:

"But why this visit, sire? What can monsieur the chancellor have to say to me that your majesty could not say yourself?"

The King turned upon his heel without reply, and almost at the same instant the captain of the guards, M. de Guitant, announced the visit of monsieur the chancellor.

When the chancellor appeared, the King had already gone out by another door.

The Queen was still standing when he entered, but scarcely had she perceived him than she reseated herself in her fauteuil and made a sign to her women to resume their cushions and stools, and, with an air of supreme hauteur, said:

"What do you desire, monsieur, and with what object do you present yourself here?"

"To make, madame, in the name of the King, and without

prejudice to the respect which I have the honour to owe to your majesty, a close perquisition into all your papers."

"How, monsieur! a perquisition into my papers!—mine!"

"Be kind enough to pardon me, madame; but in this circumstance I am but the instrument which the King employs."

"Examine, then, monsieur; I am a criminal, as it appears. Estefana, give the keys of my tables and my secretaries."

For form's sake, the chancellor paid a visit to the pieces of furniture named, but he knew that it was not in a piece of furniture that the Queen would place the important letter she had written in the course of the day.

When the chancellor had opened and shut twenty times the drawers of the secretaries, it became necessary to come to the conclusion of the affair—that is to say, to search the Queen herself. The chancellor advanced, therefore, towards Anne of Austria, and, with a very perplexed and embarrassed air—

"And now," said he, "it remains for me to make the principal perquisition."

"What is that?" asked the Queen, who did not understand, or, rather, was not willing to understand.

"His majesty is certain that a letter has been written by you in the course of the day; he knows that it has not yet been sent to its address. This letter is not in your table drawers, nor in your secretary; and yet this letter must be somewhere."

"Would you dare to lift your hand to your Queen?" said Anne of Austria, drawing herself up to her full height, and fixing her eyes upon the chancellor with an expression almost threatening.

"I am a humble subject of the King, madame, and all that his majesty commands, I shall do."

"Well, that's true!" said Anne of Austria; "and the spies of the Cardinal have served him faithfully. I have written a letter today; that letter is not yet gone. The letter is here."

And the Queen laid her beautiful hand on her bosom.

"Then give it to me, madame," said the chancellor.

"I will give it to none but the King, monsieur," said Anne.

"If the King had desired that the letter should be given to him, madame, he would have demanded it of you himself, and if you do not give it up—"

"Well?"

"He has, then, charged me to take it from you."

"How! what do you say?"

"That my orders go far, madame; and that I am authorized to seek for the suspected paper, even on the person of your majesty."

"What horror!" cried the Queen.

"Be kind enough, then, madame, to act more compliantly."

"This conduct is infamously violent!"

"The King commands it, madame; excuse me."

"I will not suffer it! no, no, I would rather die!" cried the Queen.

The chancellor made a profound reverence; then he summoned his resolution, and stretched forth his hands towards the place where the Queen had acknowledged the paper was to be found.

Anne of Austria made one step backward, became so pale that it might be said she was dying, and, leaning with her left hand, to keep herself from falling, upon a table behind her, she with her right hand drew the paper from her bosom, and held it out to the keeper of the seals.

"There, monsieur, there is that letter!" cried the Queen, with a broken and trembling voice; "take it, and deliver me from your odious presence."

The chancellor took the letter, bowed to the ground, and retired.

The door was scarcely closed upon him, when the Queen sank, half-fainting, into the arms of her women.

The chancellor carried the letter to the King, without having read a single word of it. The King took it with a trembling hand, looked for the address, which was wanting, became very pale, opened it slowly, then, seeing by the first words that it was addressed to the King of Spain, he read it rapidly.

It was nothing but a plan of an attack against the Cardinal. The Queen pressed her brother, the King of Spain, and the Emperor of Austria to appear to be wounded, as they really were, by the policy of Richelieu, the eternal object of which was the abasement of the house of Austria; to declare war against France, and as a condition of peace, to insist upon the dismissal of the Cardinal; but as to love, there was not a single word about it in all the letter.

The King, quite delighted, inquired if the Cardinal was still at the Louvre; he was told that his eminence awaited the orders of his majesty in the business cabinet.

The King went straight to him.

"There, duke," said he, "you were right, and I was wrong: the whole intrigue is political, and there is not the least question of love in this said letter. But, on the other hand, there is abundant question of you."

The Cardinal took the letter, and read it with the greatest attention; then, when he had arrived at the end of it, he read it a second time.

"Well, your majesty," said he, "you see how far my enemies go; they threaten you with two wars if you do not dismiss me. In your place, in truth, sire, I should yield to such powerful instances."

Upon which, the Cardinal, hearing the clock strike eleven, bowed lowly, demanding permission of the King to retire, and supplicating him to come to a good understanding with the Queen.

Anne of Austria, who, in consequence of the seizure of her letter, expected reproaches, was made much astonished the next day to see the King make some attempts at reconciliation with her. The King took advantage of this favourable moment to tell her he had the intention of shortly giving a fête.

On the eighth day after the scene we have described, the Cardinal received a letter with the London stamp, which only contained these lines:

I have them, but I am unable to leave London for want of money; send me five hundred pistoles, and four or five days after I receive them I shall be in Paris.

On the same day that the Cardinal received this letter, the King put his customary question to him.

Richelieu counted on his fingers, and said to himself:

"She will arrive, she says, four or five days after having received the money; it will require four or five days for the transmission of the money, four or five for her to return, that makes ten days; now, allowing for contrary winds, accidents, and a woman's weakness, we cannot make it, altogether, in less than twelve days."

"Well, monsieur le duc," said the King, "have you made your calculations?"

"Yes, sire, today is the 20th of September; the city fathers give a fête on the 3rd of October. That will fall in wonderfully well; you will not appear to have gone out of your way to please the Queen."

Then the Cardinal added:

"A propos, sire, do not forget to tell her majesty, the evening before the fête, that you should like to see how her diamond studs become her."

It was the second time the Cardinal had mentioned these diamond studs to the King. Louis XIII was struck with these repetitions, and began to fancy that this recommendation concealed some mystery.

He went then to the Queen, and, according to custom, accosted her with fresh menaces against those who surrounded her.

"Madame," said he, with dignity, "there will shortly be a ball at the Hôtel de Ville; I wish that you should appear at it in ceremonial costume, and particularly ornamented with the diamond studs which I gave you on your birthday."

"Yes, sire, I hear," stammered the Queen.

"Then that is agreed," said the King, "and that is all I had to say to you."

"But on what day will this ball take place?" asked Anne of Austria.

Louis XIII felt instinctively that he ought not to reply to that question.

"Oh! very shortly, madame," said he, "but I do not precisely recollect the date of the day; I will ask the Cardinal."

The Queen made a courtesy, less from etiquette than because her knees were sinking under her.

"I am lost," murmured the Queen. "I am lost."

Thus, whilst contemplating the misfortune which threatened her, and the abandonment in which she was left, she broke out into sobs and tears.

"Can I be of no service to your majesty?" said all at once a voice full of sweetness and pity.

The Queen turned sharply round, for there could be no deception in the expression of that voice; it was a friend who spoke thus.

In fact, at one of the doors which opened into the Queen's apartment, appeared the pretty Madame Bonacieux; she had been engaged in arranging the dresses and linen in a closet, when the King entered; she could not get out, and had heard all.

"You! oh heavens! you!" cried the Queen; "but look me in the face; I am betrayed on all sides; can I trust in you?"

"Oh! madame!" cried the young woman, falling on her knees, "upon my soul, I am ready to die for your majesty!"

This expression sprang from the very bottom of the heart, and, like the first, there was no mistaking it.

"Yes," continued Madame Bonacieux, "yes, there are traitors here; but by the holy name of the Virgin, I swear that none is more devoted to your majesty than I am. Those studs, which the King speaks of, you gave them to the Duke of Buckingham, did you not? Those studs were in a little rosewood box, which he held under his arm?"

"Oh! my God!" murmured the Queen.

"Well, those studs," continued Madame Bonacieux, "we must have them back again."

"Yes, without doubt, it must be so," cried the Queen, "but how am I to act?"

"Someone must be sent to the duke."

"But who? In whom can I trust?"

"Place confidence in me, madame; do me that honour, my Queen, and I will find a messenger."

"Do that," cried the Queen, "and you will have saved my life, you will have saved my honour."

The Queen ran to a little table, upon which were pens, ink, and paper; she wrote two lines, sealed the letter with her private seal, and gave it to Madame Bonacieux.

"And now," said the Queen, "we are forgetting one very necessary thing."

"What is that, Madame?"

"Money."

Madame Bonacieux blushed.

Anne of Austria ran to her jewel case.

"Here," said she, "here is a ring of great value, as I have been assured; it came from my brother, the King of Spain; it is mine, and I am at liberty to dispose of it. Take this ring, make money of it, and let your messenger set out."

"In an hour, you shall be obeyed, madame."

"You see the address," said the Queen, speaking so low that Madame Bonacieux could hardly hear what she said— "To Milord Duke of Buckingham, London."

"The letter shall be given to him himself."

"Generous girl," cried Anne of Austria.

Madame Bonacieux kissed the hands of the Queen, concealed the paper in the bosom of her dress, and disappeared with the lightness of a bird.

She found Bonacieux alone; the poor man was restoring order in his house, the furniture of which he had found mostly broken.

The married couple, although they had not seen each other for eight days, and that during that time serious events had taken place in which both were concerned, accosted each other with a degree of preoccupation; nevertheless, M. Bonacieux manifested real joy, and advanced towards his wife with open arms.

Madame Bonacieux presented her cheek to him.

"Let us talk a little," said she.

"Speak then."

"It is a thing of the highest interest, and upon which our future fortune perhaps depends. There is a good and holy action to be performed, monsieur, and much money to be gained at the same time."

"Much money to be gained?" said Bonacieux, protruding his lip.

"A thousand pistoles, perhaps."

"What is to be done?"

"You must set out immediately; I will give you a paper which you must not part with on any account, and which you will deliver into the proper hands."

"And where am I to go to?"

"London."

"I go to London! You are joking, I have nothing to do in London."

"An illustrious person sends you, an illustrious person awaits you; the recompense will exceed your exceptations, that is all I promise you."

"More intrigues! Nothing but intrigues! Thank you, madame, I am aware of them now; Monsieur le Cardinal has enlightened me on that head."

"The Cardinal?" cried Madame Bonacieux; "have you seen the Cardinal?"

"He sent for me," answered the mercer, proudly.

"And you went! you imprudent man!"

"Well, I can't say I had much chance in going or not going, for I was taken to him between two guards."

"He ill-treated you, then? he threatened you?"

"He gave me his hand, and he called me his friend—his

friend! do you hear that, madame? I am the friend of the great Cardinal!"

"Of the great Cardinal!"

"Yes, madame, and as his servant, I will not allow you to be concerned in plots against the safety of the state, or to assist in the intrigues of a woman who is not a Frenchwoman, and who has a Spanish heart."

"Ah! you are a cardinalist! then, monsieur, are you?" cried she, "and you serve the party who ill-treat your wife and insult your Queen?"

"Private interests are as nothing before the interests of all. I am for those who save the state," said Bonacieux, emphatically.

"And what do you know about the state you talk of?" said Madame Bonacieux, shrugging her shoulders. "Be satisfied with being a plain, straightforward bourgeois, and turn your attention to that side which holds out the greatest advantages."

"Eh! eh!" said Bonacieux, slapping a plump, round bag, which returned a sound of money; "what do you think of this, madame preacher?"

"Where does that money come from—from the Cardinal?"

"From him, and from my friend the Count de Rochefort."

"The Count de Rochefort! why, it was he who carried me off!"

"Perhaps it was, madame."

"And you receive money from that man!"

"Did you not yourself tell me that that carrying off was entirely political?"

"Yes, but that event had for its object to make me betray my mistress."

"Madame," replied Bonacieux, "your august mistress is a perfidious Spaniard, and what the Cardinal does is well done."

"Monsieur," said the young woman, "I know you to be cowardly, avaricious, and weak, but I never till now believed you to be infamous!"

"Madame, what is that you say?"

"I say you are a miserable mean creature!" continued Madame Bonacieux, who saw she was regaining some little influence over her husband.

"But what do you require of me, then? come, let us see!"

"I have told you: you must set out instantly, monsieur; you

must accomplish loyally the commission with which I deign to charge you, and on that condition I pardon everything, I forget everything, and still further,"—and she held out her hand to him—"I give you my love again."

"At least you should tell me what I should have to do in London," replied Bonacieux, who remembered a little too late that Rochefort had desired him to endeavour to obtain his wife's secrets.

"It is of no use for you to know anything about it," said the young woman, whom an instinctive mistrust now impelled to draw back; "it was about one of those purchases that interest women, a purchase by which much might have been gained."

But the more the young woman excused herself, the more important Bonacieux conceived the secret to be, which she declined to communicate to him. He resolved, then, that instant to hasten to the residence of the Count de Rochefort, and tell him that the Queen was seeking for a messenger to send to London.

"Pardon me for leaving you, my dear Madame Bonacieux," said he; "but not knowing you would come to see me, I had made an engagement with a friend; I shall soon return, and if you will wait only a few minutes for me, as soon as I have concluded my business with that friend, as it is growing late, I will come and conduct you back to the Louvre."

"Very well; I shall expect you. You are not angry with me?"

"Who, I?—Oh! not the least in the world."

Bonacieux kissed his wife's hand and set off at a quick pace.

"Well!" said Madame Bonacieux when her husband had shut the street door, and she found herself alone, "there wanted nothing to complete that poor creature but being a cardinalist! Ah! Monsieur Bonacieux! I never did love you much, but now, it is worse than ever: I hate you! and by my word, you shall pay for this!"

At the moment she spoke these words a rap on the ceiling made her raise her head, and a voice which reached her through the plaster, cried:

"Dear Madame Bonacieux, open the little passage-door for me, and I will come down to you."

VIII

"Ah! madame," said D'Artagnan, as he entered by the door which the young woman had opened for him, "allow me to tell you that you have a bad sort of a husband there!"

"You have then overheard our conversation?" asked Madame Bonacieux, eagerly, and looking at D'Artagnan with much uneasiness.

"The whole of it."

"And what did you understand by what you heard us say?"

"That the Queen wants a brave, intelligent, devoted man to make a journey to London for her. I have, at least, two of the qualities you stand in need of,—and here I am."

Madame Bonacieux made no reply, but her heart beat with joy, and secret hope shone in her eyes.

"And what pledge can you give me," asked she, "if I consent to confide this message to you?"

"I am an honourable man."

"Listen," said she, "I yield to your assurance. But I swear to you, before God who hears us, that if you betray me, and my enemies pardon me, I will kill myself, whilst accusing you of my death."

"And I, I swear to you before God, madame," said D'Artagnan, "that if I am taken whilst accomplishing the orders you give me, I will die sooner than do anything, or say anything that may compromise any one."

Then the young woman confided to him the secret of her Queen.

This was their mutual declaration of love.

D'Artagnan was radiant with joy and pride. Confidence and love made him a giant.

"I will go," said he, "I will go at once."

"You have, perhaps, no money?"

"Perhaps is too much," said D'Artagnan, smiling.

"Then," replied Madame Bonacieux, opening a cupboard

and taking from it the very bag which half an hour before her husband had caressed so affectionately, "take this bag."

"The Cardinal's!" cried D'Artagnan, breaking into a loud laugh.

"The Cardinal's," replied Madame Bonacieux.

"Pardieu!" cried D'Artagnan, "it will be a doubly amusing affair to save the Queen with the Cardinal's money!"

"You are an amiable and a charming young man!" said Madame Bonacieux; "Be assured you will not find her majesty ungrateful."

"Oh! I am already more than recompensed!" cried D'Artagnan. "I love you; you permit me to tell you that I do; that is already more happiness than I dared to hope for."

"Silence!" said Madame Bonacieux, starting.

"What!"

"Some one is talking in the street."

"It is the voice of—"

"Oh my husband! Oh! yes; I recognized it!"

D'Artagnan ran to the door and drew the bolt.

"He shall not come in before I am gone," said he; "and when I am gone, you can open the door for him."

"But I ought to be gone, too. And the disappearance of this money, how am I to justify it, if I am here?"

"Then you must come up into my room."

"Ah!" said Madame Bonacieux, "you speak that in a tone that terrifies me!"

"In my apartment you will be as safe as in a temple; I give you my word of a gentleman."

D'Artagnan drew back the bolt with precaution, and both, light as shadows, glided through the interior door into the passage, ascended the stairs as quietly as possible, and entered D'Artagnan's apartment.

Once in his apartment, for greater security, the young man barricaded the door. They both went up to the window, and, through a slit in the shutter, they saw M. Bonacieux talking with a man in a cloak.

It was the man of Meung.

D'Artagnan drew near the window and listened.

M. Bonacieux had opened his door, and seeing the apartment empty, had returned to the man in the cloak; whom he had left alone for an instant.

"She is gone," said he; "she must be gone back to the Louvre."

"You are sure," replied the stranger, "that she did not suspect the intention you went out with?"

"No," replied Bonacieux, with a self-sufficient air, "she is too superficial a woman."

"Never mind; let us walk into your apartment; we shall be better there than in the doorway."

D'Artagnan raised the three or four boards, spread a carpet, went down on his knees, and made a sign to Madame Bonacieux to do as he did, stooping down towards the opening.

"You are sure there is nobody there?" said the unknown.

"I will answer for it," said Bonacieux.

"Are you sure, that in her conversation with you, your wife mentioned no proper names?"

"No; she only told me she wished to send me to London, to further the interests of an illustrious personage."

"Oh! the traitor!" murmured Madame Bonacieux.

"Never mind," continued the man in the cloak; "It was very silly of you not to have feigned to accept the mission; you would now be in possession of the letter; the state, which is now threatened, would be safe; and you—"

"Be satisfied," replied Bonacieux; "my wife adores me, and there is still plenty of time. I will go to the Louvre, I will ask for Madame Bonacieux. I will tell her I have reflected upon the matter, I will renew the affair, I will obtain the letter, and I will run directly to the Cardinal's."

"Well! begone then! make all possible haste; I will shortly come back to learn the result of your plan."

"Now he is gone, it is your turn to set out," said Madame Bonacieux; "courage, my friend."

D'Artagnan went straight to the hotel of M. de Tréville. He had reflected that in a few minutes the Cardinal would be warned by this cursed unknown, who appeared to be his agent, and he judged, with reason, he had not a moment to lose.

"Did you ask for me, my young friend?" said M. de Tréville.

"Yes, monsieur," said D'Artagnan, "you will pardon me, I hope, for having disturbed you, when you know the importance of my business."

"Speak then, I am attentive."

"It concerns nothing less," said D'Artagnan, lowering his voice, "than the honour, perhaps the life, of the Queen."

"What do you say?" asked M. de Tréville, glancing round to see if they were alone.

"I wish you to obtain for me, from M. des Essarts, leave of absence for a fortnight."

"You are leaving Paris?"

"I am going on a mission."

"May you tell me whither?"

"To London.".

"Has anyone an interest in preventing your arrival there?"

"The Cardinal, I believe, would give anything in the world to prevent my success."

"You may take my word," continued Tréville, "in enterprises of this kind, in order that one may arrive, four must set out."

"Ah! you are right, monsieur," said D'Artagnan; "Athos, Porthos, and Aramis."

"I can send to each of them leave of absence for a fortnight, that is all: Athos, whose wound still gives him inconvenience, to go to the waters of Forges; to Porthos and Aramis to accompany their friend, whom they are not willing to abandon in such a painful position."

"Thanks, monsieur! you are a hundred times kind!"

D'Artagnan bowed to M. de Tréville, who held out his hand to him; D'Artagnan pressed it with a respect mixed with gratitude.

His first visit was for Aramis.

After the two friends had been chatting a few instants, a servant from M. de Tréville entered, bringing a sealed packet.

"What is that?" asked Aramis.

"The leave of absence monsieur had asked for," replied the lackey.

"For me! I have asked for no leave of absence!"

"Hold your tongue, and take it," said D'Artagnan. "And you, my friend, there is a demi-pistole for your trouble; you will tell M. de Tréville that M. Aramis is very much obliged to him. Go."

The lackey bowed the ground and departed.

"What does all this mean?" asked Aramis.

"Pack up all you want for a journey of a fortnight, and follow me."

"I am ready to follow you. You say we are going—"

"To Athos's residence, now, and if you will come thither, I beg you to make haste, for we have lost much time already."

Both soon arrived at Athos's dwelling.

They found him holding his leave of absence in one hand, and M. de Tréville's note in the other.

"Can you explain to me what this leave of absence and this letter, which I have just received mean?" said the astonished Athos:—'My dear Athos; I wish, as your health absolutely requires it, that you should rest for a fortnight. Go, then, and take the waters of Forges, or any that may be more agreeable to you, and re-establish yourself as quickly as possible,— Your affectionate De Tréville.' "

"Well, this leave of absence and that letter mean that you must follow me, Athos."

"In the King's service?"

"Either the King's or the Queen's; are we not their majesties' servants?"

At that moment Porthos entered.

"Pardieu!" said he; "here is a strange thing that has happened! Since when, I wonder, in the musketeers, did they grant men leave of absence without its being asked for?"

"Since," said D'Artagnan, "they have friends who ask it for them."

"Ah, ah!" said Porthos, "it appears there's something fresh afoot?"

"Yes, we are going—" said Aramis.

"To London, gentlemen," said D'Artagnan.

"To London!" cried Porthos; "and what the devil are we going to do in London?"

"That is what I am not at liberty to tell you, gentlemen; you must trust me."

"But, in order to go to London, a man should have some money; and I have none."

"Nor I," said Aramis.

"Nor I," said Porthos.

"Well, I have," added D'Artagnan, pulling out his treasure from his pocket, and placing it on the table. "There are in this bag three hundred pistoles. Let each take seventy-five, which will be quite enough to take us to London and back. Besides we may be sure that all of us will not arrive at London."

"Why so?"

"Because, according to all probability, some of us will be left on the road."

"What is this, then, a campaign upon which we are entering?"

"And a most dangerous one, I give you fair notice."

"Ah! ah! but if we do risk being killed," said Porthos, "at least I should like to know what for."

"Is the King accustomed to give you such reasons? No, he says to you, very simply: 'Gentlemen, there is fighting going on in Gascony or in Flanders; go and fight.'"

"D'Artagnan is right," said Athos; "here are our three leaves of absence, which come from M. de Tréville; and here are three hundred pistoles, which come from I don't know where. D'Artagnan, I am ready to follow you."

"And I," said Porthos.

"And I, also," said Aramis.

"And, now, when are we to go?" asked Athos.

"Immediately," replied D'Artagnan; "we have not a minute to lose."

At two o'clock in the morning, our four adventurers left Paris. The lackeys followed, armed to the teeth.

All went well till they arrived at Chantilly, which place they reached about eight o'clock in the morning. They stood in need of breakfast; and alighted at the door of an auberge, recommended by a sign representing St. Martin giving half his cloak to a poor man.

They entered the common room and placed themselves at table. A gentleman, who had just arrived, was seated at the same table. He opened the conversation by talking of rain and fine weather.

But at the moment Mousqueton came to announce that the horses were ready, the stranger proposed to Porthos to drink to the health of the Cardinal. Porthos replied that he asked no better, if the stranger in his turn, would drink to the health of the King. The stranger cried that he acknowledged no other king than his eminence. Porthos told him he was drunk, and the stranger drew his sword.

"You have committed a piece of folly," said Athos, "but it can't be helped; there is no drawing back: kill the fellow, and rejoin us as soon as you can."

And all three mounted their horses, and set out at a good pace, whilst Porthos was promising his adversary to perforate him with all the thrusts known in the fencing schools.

"There goes one!" cried Athos, at the end of five hundred paces.

And the travellers continued their route.

A league from Beauvais, where the road was confined between two high banks, they fell in with eight or ten men who, taking advantage of the road being unpaved in this spot, appeared to be employed in digging holes and filling up the ruts with mud.

Aramis, not liking to soil his boots with this artificial mortar, apostrophized them rather sharply. Athos wished to restrain him, but it was too late. The labourers began to jeer and by their insolence disturbed the equanimity even of the cool Athos, who urged on his horse against one of them.

The men all immediately drew back to the ditch, from which each took a concealed musket; the result was that our seven travellers were outnumbered in weapons. Aramis received a ball, which passed through his shoulder, and Mousqueton another ball which lodged in the fleshy part of his leg. Mousqueton alone fell from his horse.

"It is an ambuscade!" shouted D'Artagnan, "don't waste a charge! forward!"

Aramis, wounded as he was, seized the mane of his horse, which carried him on with the others. Mousqueton's horse rejoined them, and galloped by the side of his companions.

"That will serve us for a relay," said Athos.

"I would rather have had a hat," said D'Artagnan, "mine was carried away by a ball. By my faith, it is very fortunate that the letter was not in it."

They continued at their best speed for two hours.

The travellers had chosen cross-roads, in the hope that they might meet with less interruption; but at Crèvecoeur, Aramis declared he could proceed no farther. He every minute grew more pale, and they were obliged to support him on his horse. They lifted him off, at the door of a cabaret, left Bazin with him, and set forth again in the hope of sleeping at Amiens. They arrived there at midnight, and alighted at The Golden Lily.

The host had the appearance of as honest a man as any on earth; he received the travellers with his candlestick in one hand and his cotton night-cap in the other; he wished to lodge the two travellers each in a charming chamber, but, unfortunately, these charming chambers were at the opposite extremities of the hotel, and D'Artagnan and Athos declined them. The host replied that he had no other worthy of their excellencies; but his guests declared they would sleep in the common chamber, each upon a mattress, which might be thrown upon the ground.

At four o'clock in the morning, there was a terrible riot in the stables. Grimaud had tried to waken the stable-boys, and the stable-boys had set upon him and beaten him. When they opened the window they saw the poor lad lying senseless, with his head split by a blow with a fork-handle.

Planchet went down into the yard, and proceeded to saddle the horses. But the horses were all exhausted.

Athos and D'Artagnan went out, whilst Planchet was sent to inquire if there were not three horses to be sold in the neighbourhood. At the door stood two horses, fresh, strong and fully equipped. These would have just suited them. He asked where the masters of them were, and was informed that they had spent the night in the auberge, and were then settling with the master.

Athos went down to pay the reckoning, whilst D'Artagnan and Planchet stood at the street-door. The host was in a lower and back chamber, to which Athos was requested to go.

Athos entered without the least mistrust, and took out two pistoles to pay the bill. The host was alone, seated before his desk, one of the drawers of which was partly open. He took the money which Athos offered to him, and, after turning and turning it over and over in his hands, suddenly cried out that it was bad, and that he would have him and his companions arrested as coiners.

"You scoundrel!" cried Athos, stepping towards him. "I'll cut your ears off!"

But the host stooped, took two pistols from the half-open drawer, pointed them at Athos, and called out for help.

At the same instant, four men, armed to the teeth, entered by lateral doors, and rushed upon Athos.

"I am taken!" shouted Athos, with all the power of his lungs: "Go on, D'Artagnan! spur, spur!" and he fired two pistols.

D'Artagnan and Planchet did not require twice bidding: they unfastened the two horses that were waiting at the door, leaped upon them, buried their spurs in their sides, and set off at full gallop.

"Do you know what has become of Athos?" asked D'Artagnan of Planchet, as they galloped on.

"Ah, monsieur," said Planchet, "I saw one fall at each of his shots, and he appeared to me, through the glass door, to be fighting with his sword with the other."

"Brave Athos!" murmured D'Artagnan; "and to think that we are compelled to leave him, whilst the same fate awaits us, perhaps, two paces hence!"

At a hundred paces from the gates of Calais, D'Artagnan's horse sank under him.

Fortunately, as we have said, they were within a hundred paces of the city; they left their two nags upon the high road, and ran towards the port. Planchet called his master's attention to a gentleman who had just arrived with his lackey, and preceded them by about fifty paces. His boots were covered with dust, and he inquired if he could not instantly cross over to England.

"Nothing would be more easy," said the captain of a vessel ready to set sail; "but this morning an order arrived that no one should be allowed to cross without express permission from the Cardinal."

"I have that permission," said the gentleman, drawing a paper from his pocket; "here it is."

"Have it examined by the governor of the port," said the captain, "and give me the preference."

"Where shall I find the governor?"

"At his country house."

"Where is that situated?"

"At a quarter of a league from the city. Look, you may see it from here—at the foot of that little hill, that slated roof."

"Very well," said the gentleman.

And, with his lackey, he took the road to the governor's country-house.

D'Artagnan and Planchet followed the gentleman at a distance, not to be noticed; but when he was out of the city, D'Artagnan quickly came up with him, just as he was entering a little wood.

"Monsieur," said D'Artagnan, "you appear to be in great haste."

"No one can be more so, monsieur."

"I am sorry for that," said D'Artagnan; "for, as I am in

great haste likewise, I wished to beg you to render me a service."

"What service?"

"Well, then, I want that order of which you are the bearer, seeing that I have not one of my own, and must have one."

"My brave young man, I will blow out your brains. Hola, Lubin! my pistols!"

"Planchet," called out D'Artagnan, "take care of the lackey; I will manage the master."

Planchet sprang upon Lubin, and, being strong and vigorous, he soon got him on the broad of his back, and placed his knees upon his breast.

Seeing this, the gentleman drew his sword, and sprang upon D'Artagnan; but he had more than he expected to deal with.

In three seconds, D'Artagnan had wounded him three times, exclaiming at each thrust:

"One for Athos! one for Porthos! and one for Aramis!"

At the third hit the gentleman fell like a log. D'Artagnan, believing him to be dead, went toward him to take the order; but the moment he reached out his hand to search for it, the wounded man, who had not dropped his sword, plunged the point in D'Artagnan's breast, crying, "One for you!"

"And one for me—the best for the last!" cried D'Artagnan, nailing him to the earth with a fourth thrust.

This time the gentleman closed his eyes and fainted. D'Artagnan searched his pockets, and took from one of them the order for the passage. It was in the name of the Count de Wardes.

Then, casting a glance on the handsome young man, who was scarcely twenty-five years of age, and whom he was leaving in his gore, deprived of sense, and perhaps dead, he gave a sigh to that unaccountable destiny which leads men to destroy each other for the interests of people who are strangers to them, and who often do not even know that they exist.

But he was soon roused from these reflections by Lubin, who uttered loud cries and screamed for help with all his might.

"Stay!" said D'Artagnan, and taking out his handkerchief, he gagged him.

"Now," said Planchet, "let us bind him to a tree."

This being properly done, they drew the Count de Wardes close to his servant; and as night was approaching, and as the wounded man and the bound man were at some little distance within the wood, it was evident they were likely to remain there till the next day.

"And now" said D'Artagnan, "to the governor's house."

And they both set forwards as fast as they could towards the country-house of the worthy functionary.

The Count de Wardes was announced, and D'Artagnan was introduced.

"You have an order, signed by the Cardinal?"

"Yes, monsieur," replied D'Artagnan; "here it is."

"Ah, ah! it is quite regular and explicit," said the governor.

"Most likely," said D'Artagnan; "I am one of his most faithful servants."

When once out, he and Planchet set off as fast as they could, and, by making a detour, avoided the wood, and re-entered the city by another gate.

He leaped, with Planchet, into the boat. And it was time; for they had scarcely sailed half a league, when D'Artagnan saw a flash and heard a detonation—it was the cannon which announced the closing of the port.

He now had leisure to examine his wound. Fortunately, it was not dangerous: the point of the sword had touched a rib and glanced along the bone, and as his shirt had stuck to the wound, he had lost only a few drops of blood.

D'Artagnan was worn out with fatigue. A mattress was laid upon the deck for him; he threw himself upon it, and fell fast asleep.

At ten o'clock the vessel cast anchor in the port of Dover, and at half-past ten D'Artagnan placed his foot on English land.

But that was not all, they had to get to London. In England the post was well served, D'Artagnan and Planchet took post-horses with a postillion, who rode before them; and in a few hours were in the capital.

D'Artagnan did not know London, he was not acquainted with one word of English; but he wrote the name of Buckingham on a piece of paper, and every one to whom he showed it pointed out to him the way to the Duke's hotel.

The Duke was at Windsor, hunting with the King.

On their arrival at the castle they inquired for the Duke, and learned that he was hawking with the King in the marshes at some distance.

They were quickly on the spot named, and Patrick, his

confidential valet, almost at the moment caught the sound of his master's voice, recalling the falcon.

"Whom must I announce to my lord duke?" asked Patrick.

"The young man who one evening sought a quarrel with him on the Pont Neuf, opposite the Samaritaine."

Patrick galloped off, reached the duke, and announced to him, in the terms directed, that a messenger awaited him.

Buckingham at once remembered the circumstance, and suspecting that something was going on in France, rode straight up to D'Artagnan, Patrick discreetly keeping in the background.

"No misfortune has happened to the Queen?" cried Buckingham, the instant he came up, throwing all his fear and love into the question.

"I believe not; nevertheless, I believe she is in some great peril from which your grace alone can extricate her."

"I!" cried Buckingham. "What is it? I should be but too happy to render her any service! Speak! Speak!"

"Take this letter," said D'Artagnan.

"This letter! from whom does this letter come?"

"From her majesty, as I think."

"From her majesty!" said Buckingham, becoming so pale, that D'Artagnan feared he would faint,—and he broke the seal.

"What is this rent?" said he, showing D'Artagnan a place, where it had been pierced through.

"Ah! ah!" said D'Artagnan. "I did not see that; it was the sword of the Count de Wardes that made that hole when he ran it into my breast."

"Are you wounded?" asked Buckingham, as he opened the letter.

"Oh! nothing! milord, only a scratch," said D'Artagnan.

"Just Heavens! What have I read!" cried the Duke. "Patrick, remain here, or rather join the King, wherever he may be, and tell his majesty that I hereby beg him to excuse me, but an affair of the greatest importance calls me to London. Come, monsieur, come!" and both set off towards the capital at full gallop.

IX

On entering the court of his hotel, Buckingham sprang from his horse. He passed through several apartments and arrived at length in a bed-chamber which was at once a miracle of taste and of splendour. In the alcove of this chamber was a door practised in the tapestry, which the Duke opened with a small gold key, which he wore suspended from his neck by a chain of the same metal. From discretion D'Artagnan remained behind; but at the moment of Buckingham's passing through the door, he turned round, and seeing the hesitation of the young man,—

"Come in! come in!" cried he, "and if you have the good fortune to be admitted to her majesty's presence, tell her what you have seen."

Encouraged by this invitation, D'Artagnan followed the Duke, who closed the door after them.

He found himself with the Duke in a small chapel covered with a tapestry of Persian silk worked with gold, and brilliantly lit with a number of wax lights. Over a species of altar, and beneath a canopy of blue velvet, surmounted by white and red plumes, was a full-length portrait of Anne of Austria, so perfect that D'Artagnan uttered a cry of surprise on beholding it.

Upon the altar, and beneath the portrait, was the casket containing the diamond studs.

The Duke approached the altar, fell on his knees as a priest might have done before a crucifix, and opened the casket.

"There," said he, drawing from the casket a large bow of blue ribbon all sparkling with diamonds; "here are the precious studs. The Queen gave them to me, the Queen requires them back again; her will be done, like that of God, in all things."

All at once he uttered a terrible cry.

"What is the matter?" exclaimed D'Artagnan, anxiously, "what has happened to you, milord?"

"All is lost!" cried Buckingham, turning as pale as death: "two of the studs are wanting! there are but ten of them!"

"Can you have lost them, milord, or do you think they have been stolen?"

"They have been stolen!" replied the Duke, "and it is the Cardinal who has dealt me this blow. See, the ribbons which held them have been cut with scissors."

"If milord suspects that they have been stolen—perhaps the person who stole them still has them."

"Let me reflect," said the Duke—"The only time I wore these studs was at a ball given by the King, a week ago, at Windsor. The Countess de Winter, with whom I had had a quarrel, became reconciled to me at that ball. That reconciliation was nothing but the vengeance of a jealous woman. The woman is an agent of the Cardinal's."

"Patrick!" cried the Duke, opening the door of the chapel, "Patrick!"

His valet, who had that moment returned, appeared at his call.

"My jeweller and my secretary."

The valet de chambre went out with a mute promptitude that showed he was accustomed to obey implicitly and without reply.

But although the jeweller had been mentioned first, it was the secretary that first made his appearance, simply because he lived in the hotel. He found Buckingham seated at a table in his bed-chamber, writing orders with his own hand.

"Master Jackson," said he, "go instantly to the lord chancellor and tell him that I desire him to execute these orders."

"But, my lord, if the lord chancellor interrogates me upon the motives which may have led your grace to adopt such an extraordinary measure, what reply shall I make?"

"That such is my pleasure, and that I answer for my will to no man."

"Will that be the answer," replied the secretary, smiling, "which he must transmit to his majesty, if, by chance, his majesty should have the curiosity to know why no vessel is to leave any of the ports of Great Britain?"

"You are right, Master Jackson," replied Buckingham. "He will say, in that case, to the King, that I am determined on war, and that this measure is my first act of hostility against France."

The secretary bowed and retired.

D'Artagnan realized by what fragile and unknown threads the destinies of nations and the lives of men are sometimes suspended.

He was lost in these reflections when the goldsmith entered.

"Master O'Reilly," said the Duke to him, leading him into the chapel, "look at these diamond studs, and tell me what they are worth apiece."

The goldsmith cast a glance at the elegant manner in which they were set, calculated, one with another, what the diamonds were worth, and without hesitation:

"Fifteen hundred pistoles, each, my lord," replied he.

"How many days would it require to make two studs exactly like them? You see there are two wanting."

"A week, my lord."

"I will give you three thousand pistoles each for two, if I can have them by the day after tomorrow."

"My lord, you shall have them."

Buckingham assigned D'Artagnan a chamber adjoining his own. He wished to have the young man at hand, not that he at all mistrusted him, but for the sake of having some one to whom he could constantly talk about the Queen.

On the day after the morrow, by eleven o'clock, the two diamond studs were finished, and they were so completely imitated, so perfectly alike, that Buckingham could not tell the new ones from the old ones, and the most practised in such matters would have been deceived as he was.

He immediately called D'Artagnan.

"Here," said he to him, "are the diamond studs that you came to fetch, and be my witness that I have done all that human power could do."

"Be satisfied, milord; I will tell all that I have seen. But does your grace mean to give me the studs without the casket?"

"The casket would only encumber you. You will say that I keep it."

"I will perform your commission, word for word, milord."

"And now," resumed Buckingham, looking earnestly at the young man, "how shall I ever acquit myself of the debt I owe you?"

"Let us understand each other, milord," replied D'Artagnan. "I am in the service of the King and Queen of France. What I have done then has been for the Queen, and not for your grace at all."

"I understand," said the Duke, smiling.

D'Artagnan bowed to the Duke and was retiring.

"Well! you are going away in that manner? But where? and how?"

"That's true!"

"Go to the port, ask for the brig *Sund*, and give this letter to the captain; he will convey you to a little port, where certainly you are not expected, and which is ordinarily only frequented by fishermen."

"What is the name of that port?"

"Saint-Valery; but listen. When you have arrived there, you will go to a mean auberge, without a name and without a sign, a mere fisherman's hut. You cannot be mistaken, there is but one."

"And then?"

"You will ask for the host, and will repeat to him the word—Forward."

"Which means?"

"In French, en avant! that is the password. He will give you a ready-saddled horse, and will point out to you the road you are to take. You will find in this manner four relays on your route. If you will give, at each of these relays, your address in Paris, the four horses will follow you thither. The horses are equipped for the field. However proud you may be, you will not refuse to accept one of them, and to request your three companions to accept the others."

"Yes, milord, I accept them," said D'Artagnan, "and, if it please God, we will make a good use of your presents."

"Well, now, your hand, young man."

D'Artagnan bowed to the Duke and made his way as quickly as possible to the port. The next day, about nine o'clock in the morning he landed at St. Valery. D'Artagnan went instantly in search of the auberge, and easily discovered it by the riotous noise which resounded from it.

D'Artagnan made his way through the crowd, advanced toward the host, and pronounced the word, "Forward!"

The host instantly made him a sign to follow him, went out with him by a door which opened into a yard, led him to the stable, where a ready-saddled horse awaited him, and asked him if he stood in need of anything else.

"I want to know the route I am to follow," said D'Artagnan.

"Go from hence to Blangy, and from Blangy to Neufchâtel. You will find, as you have done here, a horse ready-saddled."

"Have I anything to pay?" demanded D'Artagnan.

"Everything is paid," replied the host, "and liberally."

D'Artagnan set off at full speed, and at nine o'clock galloped into the yard of M. de Tréville's hotel. He had performed nearly sixty leagues in little more than twelve hours.

M. de Tréville received him as if he had seen him that same morning; only, when pressing his hand a little more warmly than usual, he informed him that the company of M. des Essarts was on duty at the Louvre, and that he might repair at once to his post.

On the morrow, nothing was talked of in Paris but the ball which the city fathers of Paris were to give to the King and Queen.

At nine o'clock, Madame la Première Présidente arrived. As, next to the Queen, this was the most considerable personage of the fête, she was received by the city gentlemen and placed in a box opposite to that which the Queen was to occupy.

At midnight, great cries and loud acclamations were heard; it was the King. His majesty, in full dress, was accompanied by his courtiers. Everybody observed that the King looked pale and preoccupied.

Before entering his closet the King desired to be informed the moment the Cardinal arrived.

The Queen entered the great hall; and it was remarked that, like the King, she looked pale, and moreover, fatigued.

At the moment she entered, the curtain of a small gallery which to that time had been closed, was drawn, and the long face of the Cardinal appeared, he being dressed as a Spanish cavalier. His eyes were fixed upon those of the Queen, and a smile of terrible joy passed over his lips—the Queen did not wear her diamond studs.

The Queen remained for a short time to receive the compliments of the city gentlemen and to reply to the salutations of the ladies.

All at once the King appeared at one of the doors of the hall. The Cardinal was speaking to him in a low voice.

The King made his way through the crowd without a mask, and the ribbons of his doublet scarcely tied; he went straight to the Queen, and in an altered voice, said:

"Why, madame, have you not thought proper to wear your diamond studs, when you know it would have given me so much gratification?"

The Queen cast a glance around her, and saw the Cardinal behind, with a diabolical smile on his countenance.

"Sire," replied the Queen, with a faltering voice, "because in the midst of such a crowd as this, I feared some accident might happen to them."

"And you were wrong, madame! if I made you that present it was that you might adorn yourself with them. I tell you again, you were wrong."

"Sire," said the Queen, "I can send for them to the Louvre, where they are, and thus your majesty's wishes will be complied with."

."Do so, madame! do so, and that at the quickest; for within an hour the ballet will commence."

The Queen bent in token of submission, and followed the ladies who were to conduct her to her closet. On his part, the King returned to his.

The Cardinal drew near to the King, and placed in his hand a small casket. The King opened it, and found in it two diamonds.

"What does this mean?" demanded he of the Cardinal.

"Nothing," replied the latter; "only, if the Queen has the studs, of which I very much doubt, count them, sire, and if you only find ten, ask her majesty who can have stolen from her the two studs that are here."

The King looked at the Cardinal as if to interrogate him, but he had not time to address any question to him: a cry of admiration burst from every mouth. If the King appeared to be the first gentleman of his kingdom, the Queen was, without doubt, the most beautiful woman in France. She was in the full splendor of her beauty. Her carriage was that of a goddess; her eyes, which cast the brilliancy of emeralds, were full of sweetness and majesty. Her mouth was small and rosy, lovely in its smile but profoundly disdainful in contempt. Her hands and arms were of surpassing beauty, all the poets of the time singing them as incomparable. Her chestnut hair admirably set off her face.

She wore a beaver hat with blue feathers, a surtout of gray-pearl velvet fastened with diamond clasps, and a petticoat of blue satin, embroidered with silver. On her left shoulder sparkled the diamond studs, on a bow of the same color as the plumes and the petticoat.

The King trembled with joy and the Cardinal with vexation; nevertheless, distant as they were from the Queen, they could not count them; the Queen had the studs; the only question was, had she ten or twelve?

"I thank you, madame," said the King, "for the deference you have shown to my wishes, but I think you want two of the studs, and I bring them back to you."

At these words he held out to the Queen the two studs the Cardinal had given him.

"How, sire!" cried the young Queen, affecting surprise, "you are giving me then two more; but then I shall have fourteen!"

In fact, the King counted them, and the twelve studs were all on her majesty's shoulder.

The King called the Cardinal to him.

"What does this mean, Monsieur the Cardinal?" asked the King in a severe tone.

"This means, sire," replied the Cardinal, "that I was desirous of presenting her majesty with these two studs, and that not daring to offer them myself, I adopted these means of inducing her to accept them."

"And I am the more grateful to your eminence," replied Anne of Austria, with a smile that proved she was not the dupe of this ingenious piece of gallantry, "from being certain these two studs have cost you as dearly as all the others cost his majesty."

Then, after bowing to the King and the Cardinal, the Queen resumed her way to the chamber in which she had dressed, and where she was to take off her ball costume.

The Queen had just regained her chamber, and D'Artagnan was about to retire, when he felt his shoulder lightly touched; he turned round, and saw a young woman who made him a sign to follow her. The face of this young woman was covered with a black velvet mask, but, he at once recognized the light and intelligent Madame Bonacieux.

On the evening before, they had scarcely seen each other

for a moment. The haste which the young woman was in, to convey to her mistress the excellent news of the happy return of her messenger, prevented the two lovers from exchanging more than a few words. D'Artagnan then followed Madame Bonacieux, moved by a double sentiment, love and curiosity. She made a fresh sign of silence, and opened a door concealed by a tapestry.

D'Artagnan remained for a moment motionless, asking himself where he could be; but soon a ray of light which penetrated through the chamber, together with the warm and perfumed air which reached him from the same aperture, the conversation of two or three ladies, in a language at once respectful and elegant, and the word "majesty" two or three times repeated, indicated clearly that he was in a closet attached to the Queen's chamber.

At length a hand and an arm, surpassingly beautiful in their form and whiteness, glided through the tapestry. D'Artagnan, at once, comprehended that this was his recompense; he cast himself upon his knees, seized the hand, and touched it respectfully with his lips; then the hand was withdrawn, leaving in his an object which he perceived to be a ring; the door immediately closed, and D'Artagnan found himself again in complete darkness.

D'Artagnan placed the ring on his finger and again waited: it was evident that all was not yet over. After the reward of his devotion that of his love was to come.

The sound of voices diminished by degrees in the adjoining chamber; the company was then heard departing; then the door of the closet was opened, and Madame Bonacieux entered quickly.

"You at last?" cried D'Artagnan.

"Silence!" said the young woman, placing her hand upon his lips; "Silence! and begone the same way you came!"

"But where and when shall I see you again?" cried D'Artagnan.

"A note which you will find at home will tell you. Begone! begone!"

X

D'Artagnan ran home immediately, and although it was
three o'clock in the morning, and he had some of the worst
reputed quarters of Paris to pass through, he met with no
misadventure.

Planchet opened the door to him.

"Has anyone brought a letter for me?" asked D'Artagnan
eagerly.

"I found a letter upon the green tablecover in your bed-
chamber."

Whilst Planchet was saying this, the young man had darted
into his chamber, and seized and opened the letter; it was
from Madame Bonacieux, and was conceived in these terms:

> There are many thanks to be offered to you, and to
> be transmitted to you. Be this evening about ten o'clock
> at St. Cloud, in front of the pavilion built at the corner
> of the hotel of M. d'Estrees.—C.B.

At nine o'clock, D'Artagnan crossed the quays, went out by
the gate of La Conférence, and proceeded along the road,
much more beautiful then than it is now, which leads to St.
Cloud.

As long as he was in the city, Planchet kept at the respectful distance he had imposed upon himself; but as soon as the
road began to be more lonely and dark, he drew softly
nearer; so that when they entered the Bois de Boulogne, he
found himself riding quite naturally side by side with his master.

"Well, Master Planchet! what is the matter with us now?"

"Are we going to continue this pace all night?" asked Planchet.

"No, for you, on your part, are at your journey's end. You

can go into one of those cabarets that you see yonder, and be waiting for me at the door by six o'clock in the morning."

In the meantime, D'Artagnan, who had plunged into a by-path, continued his route, and gained the place appointed, and as no signal had been given him by which to announce his presence, he waited.

D'Artagnan waited half an hour without the least impatience, his eyes fixed upon that charming little abode of which he could perceive a part of the ceiling with its gilded mouldings, attesting the elegance of the rest of the apartment.

The belfry of St. Cloud struck half-past ten.

This time, without at all knowing why, D'Artagnan felt a cold shiver run through his veins.

Eleven o'clock struck.

D'Artagnan began now really to fear that something had happened to Madame Bonacieux. At that moment, he thought of the trees, and as one of them drooped over the road he thought that from its branches he might succeed in getting a glimpse of the interior of the room.

The tree was easy to climb. In an instant he was among the branches and his keen eyes plunged through the transparent window into the interior of the pavilion.

It was a strange thing to find that this soft light, this calm lamp, enlightened a scene of fearful disorder; the door of the chamber had been beaten in, and hung, split in two, on its hinges; a table, which had been covered with an elegant supper, was overturned; the decanters, broken in pieces, and the fruits crushed, strewed the floor; everything in the apartment gave evidence of a violent and desperate struggle.

He hastened down into the street, with a frightful beating at his heart; he wished to see if he could find any other traces of violence.

At length D'Artagnan, in following up his researches, found near the wall a woman's torn glove.

Then D'Artagnan ran along the high road and, coming to the ferry, closely interrogated the boatman.

About seven o'clock in the evening, the boatman said he had taken over a young woman, enveloped in a black mantle, who appeared to be very anxious not to be seen; but, entirely on account of her precautions, the boatman had paid more attention to her, and discovered that she was young and pretty.

D'Artagnan then saw a silent, obscure cottage; someone from it might have seen, no doubt, and might tell of something.

No one answered to his first knocking. A silence of death reigned in the cabin as in the pavilion; the cabin, however, was his last resource; he knocked again.

At length an old, worm-eaten shutter was opened, or rather pushed ajar. Nevertheless, rapid as the movement had been, D'Artagnan had had time to get a glimpse of the head of an old man.

D'Artagnan related his history simply, with the omission of names: he told how he had an appointment with a young woman before the pavilion, and how, not seeing her come, he had climbed the linden tree, and by the light of the lamp, had seen the disorder of the chamber.

The old man listened attentively, making a sign only that it all was so; and then, when D'Artagnan had ended, he shook his head with an air that announced nothing good.

"Oh! monsieur," said the old man, "ask me nothing; for if I told you what I have seen, certainly no good would befall me."

"You have then seen something?" replied D'Artagnan.

"It was scarcely nine o'clock when I heard a noise in the street, and on coming to my door, I found that somebody was endeavouring to open it. As I am very poor, and am not afraid of being robbed, I went and opened the gate and saw three men at a few paces from it. In the shade was a carriage with two horses and a man held three saddle horses. These horses evidently belonged to the three men, who were dressed as cavaliers.

" 'Ah! my worthy gentlemen,' cried I, 'what do you want?'

" 'Have you a ladder?' said the one who appeared to be the leader of the party.

" 'Yes, monsieur, the one with which I gather my fruit.'

" 'Lend it to us, and go into your house again; there is a crown for the annoyance we have caused you.'

"After shutting the gate behind them, I pretended to return to the house, but I immediately went out at a back door, and stealing along in the shade of the hedge, I gained yonder clump of elder, from which I could hear and see everything.

"All at once great cries resounded in the pavilion, and a woman came to the window, and opened it, as if to throw herself out of it; but as soon as she perceived the other two men, she fell back and they got into the chamber.

"Then I saw no more; but I heard the noise of breaking furniture. The woman screamed and cried for help. But her cries were soon stifled; two of the men appeared, bearing the woman in their arms. The carriage went off at a quick pace, escorted by the three horsemen, and all was over; from that moment I have neither seen nor heard anything."

"Do you know anything," said D'Artagnan, "of the man who led this infernal expedition?"

"A tall, dark man, with black moustaches, dark eyes, and looked like a gentleman."

"That's the man!" cried D'Artagnan, "again he, for ever he! He is my demon."

With a heavy heart, D'Artagnan again bent his way towards the ferry. The first thing he perceived through the damp grey mist was honest Planchet, who, with the two horses in hand, awaited him at the door of a little blind cabaret.

Instead of returning directly home, D'Artagnan alighted at the door of M. de Tréville, and ran quickly up the stairs. M. de Tréville listened to the young man's account, and when D'Artagnan had finished:

"Hum!" said he, "all this savours of his eminence, a league off."

"But what is to be done?" said D'Artagnan.

"Nothing, absolutely nothing at present. Meanwhile, I have good news for you. Your three Musketeer comrades have returned to Paris safely. They await you at Aramis's apartment."

D'Artagnan thanked M. de Tréville and hastened away to meet his friends. But while passing through the Rue Ferou, he chanced to espy that same pretty face that he had first seen at the window of a carriage. It was the English Milady. The same whom he had seen conversing with the Man of Meung.

D'Artagnan followed milady, without being perceived by her; he saw her get into her carriage, and heard her order the coachman to drive to St. Germain.

It was useless to endeavour to keep pace on foot with a carriage drawn by two powerful horses. In the Rue de Seine he met with Planchet.

He ordered him to go and saddle two horses in M. de Tréville's stables.

D'Artagnan and Planchet got into the saddle, and took the road to St. Germain. Milady had spoken to the man in the black cloak, therefore she knew him. Now, in the opinion of D'Artagnan, it was certainly the man in the black cloak who had carried off Madame Bonacieux the second time, as he had carried her off the first time. Thinking of all this, and from time to time giving a touch of the spur to his horse, D'Artagnan completed his short journey, and arrived at St. Germain. He rode up a very quiet street, looking to the right and the left to see if he could catch any vestige of his beautiful Englishwoman, when from the terrace in front of a pretty house, he saw a face peep out with which he thought he was acquainted. Planchet made out who it was first.

"Eh! monsieur!" said he, addressing D'Artagnan, "don't you remember that face which is gaping about yonder?"

"No," said D'Artagnan, "and yet I am certain it is not the first time I have seen it."

"Parbleu! I believe it is not," said Planchet: "why, it is poor Lubin, the lackey of the Count de Wardes—he whom you so well accommodated a month ago, at Calais, on the road to the governor's country house!"

"So it is!" said D'Artagnan. "Do you think he would recollect you?"

"Ma foi! monsieur, he was in such trouble, that I don't think he can have retained a very clear recollection of me."

"Well, go and get into conversation with him, and make out, if you can, whether his master is dead or not."

Planchet dismounted, and went straight up to Lubin, who did not remember him, and the two lackeys began to chat with the best understanding possible; whilst D'Artagnan turned the two horses into a lane, and went round the house, coming back to watch the conference from behind a hedge of nut-trees.

At the end of an instant's observation he heard the noise of a carriage stop opposite him. He could not be mistaken—milady was in it. D'Artagnan stooped down upon the neck of his horse in order that he might see without being seen.

Milady put her charming fair head out of the window, and gave her orders to her female attendant.

The latter, a pretty girl of about twenty years of age, jumped from the step. D'Artagnan followed the soubrette with his eyes, and saw her go towards the terrace. But it happened that someone in the house called Lubin, so that Planchet remained alone, looking in all directions for his master.

The femme de chambre approached Planchet, whom she took for Lubin, and holding out a little billet to him:

"For your master," said she.

"For my master?" replied Planchet, in astonishment.

"Yes—and of consequence,—take it quickly."

Thereupon she ran towards the carriage, which had turned round towards the way it came, jumped upon the step, and the carriage drove off.

Planchet turned the billet on all sides, then met D'Artagnan, who, having seen it all, was coming to meet him.

"For you, monsieur," said Planchet, presenting the billet to the young man.

D'Artagnan opened the letter, and read these words:

> A person who takes more interest in you than she is willing to confess, wishes to know on what day it will suit you to walk in the forest? To-morrow, at the Hôtel du Champ du Drap d'Or, a lackey in black and red will wait for your reply.

"Oh! oh!" said D'Artagnan, "this is rather warm; it appears that milady and I are anxious about the health of the same person. Well, Planchet, how is the good M. de Wardes, he is not dead, then?"

"Oh no, monsieur, he is as well as a man can be with four sword-wounds in his body; for you, without question, inflicted four upon the dear gentleman, and he is still very weak, having lost almost all his blood. As I said, monsieur, Lubin did not know me, and told me our adventure from one end to the other."

"Well done, Planchet! you are the king of lackeys. Now jump up on your horse, and let us overtake the carriage."

They soon effected this. At the end of five minutes they perceived the carriage drawn up by the road-side; a cavalier, richly dressed, was close to the coach-door.

The conversation between milady and the cavalier was so animated, that D'Artagnan stopped on the other side of the carriage without anyone but the pretty soubrette being aware of his presence.

The conversation took place in English,—a language which D'Artagnan could not understand; but, by the accent, the young man plainly saw that the beautiful Englishwoman was in a great rage: she terminated it by a blow with her fan, applied with such force that the little feminine weapon flew into a thousand pieces.

The cavalier broke into a loud laugh, which appeared to exasperate milady still more.

D'Artagnan thought this was the moment to interfere; he approached the other door, and taking off his hat respectfully—

"Madame," said he, "will you permit me to offer you my services? It appears to me that this cavalier has made you very angry. Speak one word, madame, and I take upon myself to punish him for his want of courtesy."

At the first word, milady turned round, looking at the young man with astonishment; and when he had finished—

"Monsieur," said she, in very good French, "I should with great confidence place myself under your protection, if the person with whom I quarrel were not my brother."

"Ah! excuse me, then," said D'Artagnan, "you must be aware that I was ignorant of that, madame!"

"What is that stupid fellow troubling himself about?" cried the cavalier, whom milady had designated as her brother, stooping down to the height of the coach window,—"why does not he go about his own business?"

"Stupid fellow yourself!" said D'Artagnan, stooping in his turn on the neck of his horse, and answering on his side through the carriage window.

The cavalier addressed some words in English to his sister.

"I speak to you in French," said D'Artagnan; "be kind enough, then, to reply to me in the same language."

It might be thought that milady, timid as women are in general, would have interposed in this commencement of mutual provocations, in order to prevent the quarrel from going too far; but, on the contrary, she threw herself back in her carriage, and called out coolly to the coachman, "Go on—home!"

The carriage went on, and left the two men in face of each other.

The cavalier made a movement, as if to follow the carriage; but D'Artagnan caught at his bridle and stopped him.

"You see plainly that I have no sword," said the Englishman. "Do you wish to play the braggart with an unarmed man?"

"I hope you have a sword at home; but, at all events, I have two, and, if you like, I will throw with you for one of them."

"Quite unnecessary," said the Englishman; "I am well furnished with such sorts of playthings."

"Very well! my worthy gentleman," replied D'Artagnan; "pick out the longest and come and show it to me this evening."

"Where?"

"Behind the Luxembourg; that's a charming spot for such amusements as the one I propose to you."

"That will do; I will be there."

"Your hour?"

"Six o'clock."

"Apropos, you have probably one or two friends?"

"Humph! I have three who would be honoured by joining in the sport with me."

"Three! that's fortunate! That falls out oddly! Three is just my number."

"Now then, who are you?" asked the Englishman.

"I am M. D'Artagnan, a Gascon gentleman, serving in the guards, in the company of M. des Essarts. And you?"

"I am the Lord de Winter, Baron of Sheffield."

"Well, then, I am your servant, monsieur le baron," said D'Artagnan, "though you have names rather difficult to recollect."

And touching his horse with the spur, he cantered back to Paris. There to acquaint his three friends of the meeting for that evening.

XI

The hour being come, they, with their four lackeys, repaired to a spot behind the Luxembourg.

A silent party soon drew near to the same enclosure, penetrated into it, and joined the musketeers; then, according to the English custom, the presentations took place.

"But, after all this," said Lord de Winter, when the three friends had been named, "we do not know who you are; as gentlemen, we cannot fight with such; why, they are nothing but shepherds' names."

"Therefore your lordship may suppose they are only assumed names," said Athos.

"Which only gives us a greater desire to know the real ones," replied milord.

"And that is but just," said Athos, and he took aside that one of the four Englishmen with whom he was to fight, and communicated his name in a low voice.

Porthos and Aramis did the same.

"Does that satisfy you?" said Athos to his adversary; "do you think me sufficiently noble to do me the honour of crossing swords with me?"

"Yes, monsieur," said the Englishman, bowing.

"Well! now shall I tell you another thing?" said Athos coolly.

"What is that?" replied the Englishman.

"Why, that is, that you would have acted much more wisely if you had not required me to make myself known."

"Why so?"

"Because I am believed to be dead, and have reasons for wishing nobody should know I am living, so that I shall be obliged to kill you to prevent my secret getting wind."

The Englishman looked at Athos, believing that he was joking, but Athos was not joking the least in the world.

"Gentlemen," said Athos, addressing at the same time his companions and their adversaries, "are we ready?"

"Yes!" answered the Englishmen and the Frenchmen, as with one voice.

"Guard, then!" cried Athos.

And immediately eight swords glittered in the rays of the setting sun. Athos fenced with as much calmness and method as if he had been practising in a school.

Porthos, corrected, no doubt, of his too great confidence by his adventure of Chantilly, played with finesse and prudence.

Aramis, who had the third canto of his poem to finish, made all the despatch of a man very much pressed for time.

Athos killed his adversary—the sword passed through his heart.

Porthos, stretched his upon the grass, with a wound through his thigh; and as the Englishman, without making any further resistance, then surrendered his sword, Porthos took him up in his arms and carried him to his carriage.

Aramis pushed his so vigorously, that after going back fifty paces, he finished by fairly taking to his heels, and disappeared amid the hooting of the lackeys.

As to D'Artagnan, he fought purely and simply on the defensive; and when he saw his adversary pretty well fatigued with a vigorous side-thrust, he twisted the sword from his grasp, and sent it glittering into the air. The baron finding himself disarmed, gave two or three paces back, but in this movement, his foot slipped and he fell.

D'Artagnan was over him at a bound, and pointing his sword to his throat,—

"I could kill you, milord," said he to the Englishman; "you are completely at my mercy, but I spare your life for the sake of your sister."

The Englishman, delighted at having to do with a gentleman of such a kind disposition, pressed D'Artagnan in his arms and paid a thousand compliments to the three musketeers, and, as Porthos's adversary was already installed in the carriage, and as Aramis's had run away, they had nothing to think about but the defunct.

As Porthos and Aramis were undressing him in the hope of finding his wound not mortal, a large purse dropped from his clothes. D'Artagnan picked it up and held it out to Lord de Winter.

"What the devil would you have me to do with that?" said the Englishman.

"You can restore it to his family," said D'Artagnan.

"His family will care vastly about such a trifle as that! his family will inherit fifteen thousand louis a year from him; keep the purse for your lackeys."

D'Artagnan put the purse in his pocket.

"And now, my young friend, if you will permit me, I hope to give you that name," said Lord de Winter, "on this very evening, if agreeable to you, I will present you to my sister, Lady Clarik. She is not in bad odour at court, she may perhaps, on some future day, speak a word that will not prove useless to you."

D'Artagnan blushed with pleasure, and bowed a sign of assent.

Lord de Winter, on quitting D'Artagnan, gave him his sister's address; she lived, No. 6, Place Royale, then the fashionable quarter, and undertook to call and take him with him in order to introduce him. D'Artagnan appointed eight o'clock at Athos's residence.

This introduction to Lady Clarik occupied the head of our Gascon greatly. He remembered in what a strange manner this woman had been mixed up in his destiny.

D'Artagnan began by making his most splendid toilette; then returned to Athos's, and, according to custom, related everything to him.

"What!" said he, "you have just lost one woman, who, you say, was good, charming, perfect, and here you are, running headlong after another!"

D'Artagnan felt the truth of this reproach.

"I loved Madame Bonacieux with my heart, whilst I only love milady with my head," said he; "by getting introduced to her, my principal object is to ascertain what part she plays at court."

"The part she plays at court, pardieu! it is not difficult to divine that. She is some emissary of the Cardinal's."

"The devil! my dear Arthos, you view things on the dark side, methinks."

"D'Artagnan, I mistrust women; can it be otherwise! I bought my experience dearly—particularly fair women."

"Tell it, Athos, tell it."

"You particularly wish it?"

"I pray for it," replied D'Artagnan.

"One of my friends—not myself, but one of the counts of my province—at twenty-five years of age fell in love with a girl of sixteen, beautiful as fancy can paint. She lived in a small town with her brother, who was a curate. My friend, who was seigneur of the county, might have seduced her, or taken her by force, at his will. Unfortunately he was an honourable man; he married her. He took her to his chateau, and made her the first lady in the province; and it must be allowed that she supported her rank becomingly."

"Well?" asked D'Artagnan.

"Well, one day as they were hunting she fell from her horse and fainted. The count rushed to her help, cutting her laces with his poniard, and in so doing bared her shoulder. D'Artagnan," said Athos, with a maniacal burst of laughter, "guess what she had there?"

"How can I tell?"

"A *fleur-de-lis*. The angel was a demon! She had been branded for stealing the sacred vessels from a church."

"What did the count do?"

"The count was of the highest nobility. He had on his estates the right of sovereign justice. He tore the dress of the countess to pieces, tied her hands behind her, and hanged her on a tree."

"Heavens, Athos, a murder?" cried D'Artagnan.

"No less," said Athos, pale as a corpse. "That has cured me of beautiful, poetical, and loving women," he concluded, forgetting to continue the fiction of "the count" as cover for his own story. "God grant you as much!"

"Then she is dead?" stammered D'Artagnan. "And her brother?"

"I inquired after him for the purpose of hanging him too, but he had left his curacy the night before. He was doubtless the first lover and the accomplice of the lady."

"My God!" cried D'Artagnan, horrified by this relation.

Lord de Winter arrived at the appointed time. An elegant carriage waited below, and as it was drawn by two excellent horses, they were soon at the Place Royale.

Milady Clarik received D'Artagnan ceremoniously.

"You see," said Lord de Winter, presenting D'Artagnan, "a young gentleman who has held my life in his hands, and who has not abused his advantage. Thank him then, madame, if you have any affection for me."

Milady frowned slightly, a scarcely visible cloud passed over her brow.

"You are welcome, monsieur," said milady, in a voice whose singular sweetness contrasted with the symptoms of ill-humour which D'Artagnan had just remarked,—"you have today acquired eternal rights to my gratitude."

Lord de Winter went to a table upon which was a salver with Spanish wine and glasses. He filled two, and by a sign, invited D'Artagnan to drink.

D'Artagnan knew that it was considered disobliging by an Englishman to refuse to pledge him; therefore, he drew near to the table and took the second glass. He did not, however, lose sight of milady, and in a mirror perceived the change that took place in her face. Now that she believed herself to be no longer observed, a sentiment which resembled ferocity animated her countenance. She bit her handkerchief with all her might.

That pretty little soubrette that D'Artagnan had already observed, then came in; she spoke some words to Lord de Winter, in English; and he immediately requested d'Artagnan's permission to retire.

D'Artagnan exchanged a shake of the hand with Lord de Winter, and then returned to milady. Her countenance, with surprising mobility, had recovered its gracious expression, but some little red spots upon her handkerchief indicated that she had bitten her lips till the blood came.

The conversation took a cheerful turn. Milady appeared to be entirely recovered. She told D'Artagnan that Lord de Winter was her brother-in-law, and not her brother; she had married a younger brother of the family, who had left her a widow with one child. This child was the only heir to Lord de Winter, if Lord de Winter did not marry.

In addition to this, after half an hour's conversation, D'Artagnan was convinced that milady was his compatriot; she spoke French with an elegance and a purity that left no doubt on that head.

D'Artagnan was profuse in gallant speeches and protestations of devotedness. The hour for retiring arrived. D'Artagnan took leave of milady, and left the salon the happiest of men.

Upon the stairs he met the pretty soubrette, who brushed gently against him as she passed, and then, blushing to the eyes, asked his pardon for having touched him, in a voice so sweet, that the pardon was granted instantly.

D'Artagnan came again on the morrow, and was still better received than on the day before. Milady appeared to take a great interest in him, asked him whence he came, who were his friends, and whether he had not at some times thought of attaching himself to M. le Cardinal.

D'Artagnan, who was exceedingly prudent for a young man of twenty, then launched into an eulogy of his eminence and said that he should not have failed to enter the guards of the Cardinal instead of the King's guards, if he had happened to know M. de Cavois instead of M. de Tréville.

Milady changed the conversation without any appearance of affectation, and asked D'Artagnan in the most carefree manner possible, if he had never been in England.

D'Artagnan replied that he had been sent thither by M. de Tréville, to trade for a number of horses and that he had brought back four as specimens.

At the same hour as the preceding evening D'Artagnan retired. In the corridor he again met the pretty Kitty; that was the name of the soubrette. She looked at him with an expression of kindness which it was impossible to mistake. But D'Artagnan was so preoccupied by the mistress, that he remarked nothing but her.

In spite of the cries of his conscience and the wise counsels of Athos, D'Artagnan became hourly more in love with milady!

One day when he arrived, with his head in the air, and as light at heart as a man who is in expectation of a shower of gold, he found the soubrette under the gateway of the hotel; but this time the pretty Kitty was not contented with touching him as he passed; she took him gently by the hand.

"I wish to say three words to you, Monsieur le Chevalier," stammered the soubrette.

"Speak, my dear, speak," said D'Artagnan; "I am all attention."

"If Monsieur le Chevalier would follow me?" said Kitty, timidly.

"Where you please, my pretty little dear."

Kitty, who had not let go the hand of D'Artagnan, led him up a little dark, winding staircase, and opened a door.

"Come in here, Monsieur le Chevalier," said she.

"And whose chamber is this, my pretty-faced friend?"

"It is mine, Monsieur le Chevalier. You love my mistress, then, very dearly, Monsieur le Chevalier?" said she.

"Oh, more than I can say, Kitty! I am mad for her!"

Kitty breathed a second sigh.

"Alas! monsieur," said she, "that is a great pity!"

"What the devil do you see so pitiable in it?" said D'Artagnan.

"Because, monsieur," replied Kitty, "my mistress does not love you at all."

"Hein!" said D'Artagnan, "can she have charged you to tell me so?"

"Oh, no, monsieur; out of regard I have for you, I have taken upon myself to tell you so."

"I am much obliged, my dear Kitty, but for the intention only: for the information, you must agree, is not likely to be very pleasant."

"Then you don't believe me?"

"Why, I confess that, unless you give me some proof of what you advance—"

"What do you think of this?"

And Kitty drew a little note from her bosom.

"For me?" said D'Artagnan, seizing the letter.

"No; for another."

"His name! his name!" cried D'Artagnan.

"Monsieur le Comte de Wardes."

The remembrance of the scene at St. Germain presented itself to the mind of the presumptuous Gascon; as quick as thought he tore open the letter.

"Oh, good Lord! Monsieur le Chevalier," said she, "what are you going to do?"

"Who—I?" said D'Artagnan; "nothing;" and he read:

> You have not answered my first note; are you indisposed, or have you forgot the glances you favoured me with at the hall of Madame de Guise? You have an opportunity now, count; do not allow it to escape.

D'Artagnan became very pale.

"Poor, dear Monsieur D'Artagnan!" said Kitty, in a voice full of compassion, and pressing the young man's hand again.

"You pity me, my kind little creature?" said D'Artagnan.

"That I do, and with all my heart; for I know what it is to be in love."

The following scenes are from the Alexander Salkind production, "The Three Musketeers," released by 20th Century-Fox.

D'Artagnan
(Michael York)

Athos
(Oliver Reed)

Aramis
(Richard Chamberlain)

Porthos
(Frank Finlay)

D'Artagnan asks to join the King's Musketeers.

D'Artagnan's swordplay with the Musketeers interrupted by the Cardinal's henchmen.

Cardinal Richelieu (Charlton Heston)

The opulence of Louis XIII's Court.

Milady, Countess de Winter
(Faye Dunaway)

Rochefort
(Christopher Lee)

Louis XIII
(Jean-Pierre Cassel)

Anne of Austria, Queen of France
(Geraldine Chaplin)

D'Artagnan and Constance Bonacieux (Raquel Welch)
in a tender interlude.

Anne of Austria with her love,
the Duke of Buckingham (Simon Ward)

D'Artagnan duels with one of the Cardinal's men.

Athos at a crucial moment.

Aramis in action.

Aramis and Porthos.

The conspirators, Richelieu and Milady.

Their Majesties dance at the ball.

"You know what it is to be in love?" said D'Artagnan, looking at her for the first time with much attention.

"Alas! yes."

"Well, then, instead of pitying me, you would do much better to assist me in revenging myself of your mistress."

"And what sort of revenge would you take?"

"I would triumph over her, and supplant my rival."

"I will never help you in that, Monsieur le Chevalier," said Kitty, warmly.

"Why not?"

"For two reasons."

"What are they?"

"The first is, that my mistress will never love you."

"How do you know that?"

"You have offended her to the very heart."

"I?—in what can I have offended her? Speak, I beg of you!"

"I will never confess that but to the man—who should read to the bottom of my soul!"

D'Artagnan looked at Kitty for the second time. The young girl was of a freshness and beauty which many duchesses would have purchased with their coronets.

"Kitty," said he, "I will read to the bottom of your soul whenever you like; don't let that disturb you"; and he gave her a kiss, at which the poor girl became as red as a cherry.

"Oh, no," said Kitty, "it is not me you love—it is my mistress you love; you told me so only just now."

"And does that hinder you from telling me the second reason?"

"The second reason, Monsieur le Chevalier," replied Kitty, emboldened by the kiss in the first place, and still further by the expression of the eyes of the young man, "is—that in love, every one for herself!"

Then only D'Artagnan remembered the languishing glances of Kitty, her constantly meeting him in the antechamber, the corridor or on the stairs, those touches of the hand every time she did meet him, and her deep sighs.

But this time our Gascon saw at a glance all the advantage that might be derived from the love which Kitty had just confessed so innocently—or so boldly; the interception of letters addressed to the Count de Wardes, intelligences on the spot, entrance at all hours into Kitty's chamber, which was contiguous to her mistress's.

"Well," said he to the young girl, "are you willing, my dear Kitty, that I should give you a proof of that love of which you doubt?"

"What love?" asked the girl.

"Of that which I am ready to feel for you."

"And what is that proof?"

"Are you willing that I should this evening pass with you the time I generally spend with your mistress?"

"Oh yes!" said Kitty, clapping her hands, "very willing."

"Well, then, come here, my dear," said D'Artagnan, establishing himself in a fauteuil, "come, and let me tell you that you are the prettiest soubrette I ever saw!"

And he did tell her so much, and so well, that the poor girl, who asked nothing better than to believe him, did believe him.

In such conversations time passes very rapidly. Twelve o'clock struck, and almost at the same time the bell was rung in milady's chamber.

"Good God!" cried Kitty, "there is my mistress calling me! Go, go directly!"

D'Artagnan rose, took his hat as if it had been his intention to obey; then, opening quickly the door of a large closet, instead of that of the staircase, he plunged into the midst of robes and lady's dressing-gowns.

"What are you doing?" cried Kitty.

D'Artagnan, who had secured the key, shut himself up in the closet without any reply.

"Well," cried milady, in a sharp voice, "are you asleep, that you don't answer when I ring?"

And D'Artagnan heard the door of communication opened violently.

"Here I am, milady! here am I!" cried Kitty, springing forward to meet her mistress.

Both went into the bedroom, and, as the door of communication remained open, D'Artagnan could hear milady for some time scolding her maid. She was at length, however, appeased, and the conversation turned upon him whilst Kitty was assisting her mistress to undress.

"Well," said milady, "I have not seen our Gascon this evening."

"What, milady! has he not been?" said Kitty. "Can he be inconstant before being happy?"

"Oh, no; he must have been prevented by M. de Tréville or M. des Essarts. I have him safe!"

"What will you do with him, madame?"

"Oh Kitty, there is something between that man and me that he is quite ignorant of: he was very near making me lose my credit with his eminence. Oh, I will be revenged for that!"

"I thought madame loved him?"

"I love him? I detest him! A simple fool, who held the life of Lord de Winter in his hands and did not kill him, by which I missed three hundred thousand livres a year!"

D'Artagnan shuddered to his very marrow at hearing this apparently sweet creature reproach him with that sharp voice, which she took such pains to conceal in conversation, for not having killed a man whom he had seen load her with kindnesses.

"For all this," continued milady: "I should long ago have revenged myself on him, if, and I don't know why, the Cardinal had not requested me to conciliate him."

"Oh, yes; but madame has not favoured the little woman he was so fond of?"

"What! the mercer's wife of the Rue des Fossoyeurs? Has he not already forgotten she ever existed? Fine vengeance that, ma foi!"

A cold sweat broke from D'Artagnan's brow. Why, this woman was a monster!

"That will do," said milady; "go into your own room, and tomorrow endeavour again to obtain me an answer to the letter I gave you."

"For M. de Wardes?" said Kitty.

"To be sure; for M. de Wardes."

"Now, there is one," said Kitty, "who appears to me to be quite a different sort of man to that poor M. D'Artagnan."

D'Artagnan heard the door close, then the noise of two bolts by which milady fastened herself in; on her side, but as softly as possible, Kitty turned the key of the lock, and then D'Artagnan opened the closet-door.

"Oh good Lord!" said Kitty, in a low voice, "what is the matter with you? How pale you are!"

"The abominable creature!" murmured D'Artagnan.

"Silence, silence! begone!" said Kitty; "there is nothing but a wainscot between my chamber and milady's; every word that is uttered in one can be heard in the other."

"That's exactly the reason I won't go," said D'Artagnan.

"What!" said Kitty blushing.

"Or, at least, I will go—later"; and he put his arm around her waist.

D'Artagnan's love for Kitty was little more than an idea of vengeance upon milady. It must, however, be confessed, in his justification, that the first use he made of the influence he had obtained over Kitty was, to endeavour to find out what had become of Madame Bonacieux; but the poor girl swore upon the crucifix to D'Artagnan, that she was entirely ignorant on that head.

As to the cause which was near making milady lose the confidence of the cardinal, Kitty knew nothing about it; but this time D'Artagnan was better informed than she was. He suspected that it was, almost without a doubt, on account of the diamond studs.

But what was clearest in all this was that the true hatred of milady was increased by his not having killed her brother-in-law.

D'Artagnan came the next day to milady's, and finding her in a very ill-humour, had no doubt that it was having no answer from M. de Wardes that provoked her thus.

Towards the end of the evening, however, the beautiful lioness became milder, she smilingly listened to the soft speeches of D'Artagnan, and even gave him her hand to kiss.

D'Artagnan, at parting, scarcely knew what to think; but, as he was a youth not easily imposed upon, whilst continuing to pay his court to milady, he determined to carry out the little plan he had framed in his mind.

He found Kitty at the gate, and, as on the previous evening, went up to her chamber. Milady could not at all comprehend the silence of the Count de Wardes, and she ordered Kitty to come at nine o'clock in the morning to take a third letter.

D'Artagnan made Kitty promise to bring him that letter on the following morning.

At eleven o'clock Kitty came to him: she held in her hand a fresh billet from milady. This time the poor girl did not even hesitate at giving up the note to D'Artagnan; she belonged, body and soul, to her handsome soldier.

D'Artagnan opened the letter, and read as follows:

This is the third time I have written to you, to tell you that I love you. Beware that I do not write to you a fourth time, to tell you that I detest you.

If you repent of the manner in which you have acted towards me, the young girl who brings you this will tell you how a man of spirit may obtain his pardon.

D'Artagnan took a pen and wrote:

MADAME—Until the present moment, I could not believe that it was to me your two first letters were addressed, so unworthy did I feel myself of such an honour; besides, I was so seriously indisposed, that I could not, in any case, have replied to them.

But now, I am forced to believe in the excess of your kindness, since not only your letter, but your servant, assures me that I have the good fortune to be beloved by you.

She has no occasion to teach me the way in which a man of spirit may obtain his pardon; I will come and ask mine at eleven o'clock this evening.

To delay it a single day would be, in my eyes, now, to commit a fresh offence—He whom you have rendered the happiest of men,

COMTE DE WARDES

"There," said the young man, handing Kitty the letter, sealed and addressed, "give that to milady; it is the Count de Wardes' reply."

Poor Kitty became as pale as death; she suspected what the letter contained.

"Listen, my dear girl," said D'Artagnan, "you cannot but perceive that all this must end, some way or other; milady may discover that you gave the first billet to my lackey instead of to De Wardes'; that it is I who have opened the others which ought to have been opened by him; milady will then turn you out of doors, and you know she is not the woman to let her vengeance stop there."

"Alas!" said Kitty, "for whom have I exposed myself to all that?"

"For me, I well know, my sweet girl," said D'Artagnan. "But I am grateful."

"But what does this note contain?"

"Milady will tell you."

"Ah! you do not love me," cried Kitty, "and I am very wretched!"

In spite of the caresses with which D'Artagnan endeavoured to console her, Kitty wept for some time before she could be persuaded to give her mistress the note; but she yielded at last.

XII

Athos sat chewing the cud of recollections, in which the bitter somewhat predominated over the sweet, when his meditations were pleasingly interrupted by the appearance of D'Artagnan.

"This seems to have been an auspicious night with you, D'Artagnan," said Athos. "Did you visit your fascinating Englishwoman?"

"Oh yes," replied D'Artagnan, rubbing his hands; "and my revenge is complete."

"Well we know she was a spy of the Cardinal's," said Athos.

"Peste!" said D'Artagnan: "that is it. I almost trembled while I loved. But I will tell you all and you may judge for yourself." And with his usual readiness and fluency, the Gascon related to his attentive friend the adventures of the evening.

"Well, at my usual time, about nine o'clock, I presented myself. I had never seen her look handsomer.

"At ten o'clock milady began to be uneasy. She arose, walked about, sat down again. At length, as the time drew near, there was no mistaking her. I arose, took my hat, bowed upon her hand, even ventured to kiss it.

"She must love him devilishly," thought I, as I descended the stairs.

"On reaching the soubrette's little apartment, I found her seated with her head leaning on her hands, weeping bitterly.

"My heart smote me more than I like to own, but my plan lay too much at my heart.

"I had not been many minutes with Kitty before we heard milady enter her chamber, and I quickly ensconced myself in the closet.

"Milady appeared intoxicated with joy. A few minutes before the appointed hour, milady had all the lights put out in her chamber, and dismissed Kitty to hers, with an injunction to introduce the count the moment he arrived.

"You may suppose I did not keep Kitty waiting long.

"Seeing through a chink of my hiding place that all was darkness, I was at the door of milady's chamber before Kitty had closed it.

" 'What is that noise?' said milady.

" 'It is I, De Wardes,' replied I, in a suppressed voice.

" 'Well, why do you not come in?' said milady.

"I made my way into milady's dark chamber. And here, dear Athos, I must confess that I scarcely knew which predominated, love or hatred."

"Call it not love, D'Artagnan," said Athos.

"Well, call it what you will, she is intensely in earnest, as you may judge. At parting, she forced this ring upon my finger."

"Your milady's doubtless an infamous creature. But since you mentioned it, my attention has been engrossed by your ring," said Athos.

"I saw you were looking at it; it is handsome, is it not?" said D'Artagnan.

"Let me look at it," said Athos; and, as he took it and examined it, he became very pale. He tried it on his little finger, which it fitted as if made for it.

"It is impossible," said he. "How could this ring come into the possession of Lady Clarik? And yet it is difficult to suppose such a resemblance should exist between two jewels."

"Do you know this ring?" asked D'Artagnan.

"I thought I did," replied Athos; "but, no doubt, was mistaken. But stop, let me look at the ring again; the one I mentioned to you had one of its faces scratched."

Athos started. "Look," said he, "is it not strange?" and he pointed out to D'Artagnan the scratch he had remembered.

"But from whom did this ring come to you, Athos?"

"From my mother, who inherited it from her mother."

"And you—sold it?" asked D'Artagnan, hesitatingly.

"No," replied Athos, with a singular smile; "I gave it away in a love affair, as it has been given to you."

D'Artagnan became pensive in his turn. He took back the ring, but put it in his pocket, and not on his finger.

"D'Artagnan," said Athos, taking his hand, "you know I love you; if I had a son, I could not love him better. Take my advice, renounce this woman."

"You are right," said D'Artagnan. "I have done with her; she terrifies me."

"Shall you have the courage?" said Athos.

"I shall," replied D'Artagnan; "and instantly."

That next evening milady gave orders that when M. D'Artagnan came as usual, he should be immediately admitted. But he did not come.

The next morning, when Kitty presented herself at D'Artagnan's residence she was no longer joyous.

D'Artagnan asked the poor girl what was the matter with her, but she, as her only reply, drew a letter from her pocket and gave it to him.

This letter was in milady's handwriting, only this time it was addressed to M. D'Artagnan, and not to M. de Wardes.

He opened it, and read as follows:

Dear Monsieur D'Artagnan—It is wrong thus to neglect your friends, particularly at the moment you are about to leave them for so long a time. My brother-in-law and myself expected you yesterday and the day before, but in vain. Will it be the same this evening?
Your very grateful
Lady Clarik

"That's all very simple," said D'Artagnan; "I expected this letter."

"And will you go?"

"Listen to me, my dear girl," said the Gascon, who sought for an excuse in his own eyes for breaking the promise he had made Athos; "you must understand it would be impolitic not to accept such a positive invitation."

"Oh dear!" said Kitty, "you know how to represent things in such a way that you are always in the right. You are going now to pay your court to her again, and if, this time, you succeed in pleasing her in your own name and with your own face, it will be much worse than before."

D'Artagnan reassured her as well as he could, and promised to remain insensible to the seductions of milady.

He desired Kitty to tell her mistress that he could not be more grateful for her kindnesses than he was, and that he would be obedient to her orders. He did not dare to write, for fear of not being able to such experienced eyes as those of milady, to disguise his writing sufficiently.

As nine o'clock struck, D'Artagnan was at the Place Royale. It was evident that the servants who waited in the antechamber were warned, for as soon as D'Artagnan appeared, before even he had asked if milady were visible one of them ran to announce him.

"Show him in," said milady, in a quick tone, but so piercing that D'Artagnan heard her in the antechamber.

He was introduced.

"I am at home to nobody," said milady; "observe, to nobody."

The servant went out.

D'Artagnan cast an inquiring glance at milady. She was pale, and her eyes looked red, either from tears or want of sleep. The number of lights had been intentionally diminished, but the young woman could not conceal the traces of the fever which had devoured her during the last two days.

To the questions which D'Artagnan put concerning her health—

"Ill!" replied she, "very ill!"

"Then," replied he, "my visit is ill-timed."

"No, no," said milady: "Stay, Monsieur D'Artagnan, your agreeable company will divert me."

"Oh! oh!" thought D'Artagnan. "She has never been so kind before. I must be on my guard."

By degrees, milady became more communicative. She asked D'Artagnan if he had a mistress.

"Alas!" said D'Artagnan, with the most sentimental air he could assume, "can you be cruel enough to put such a question to me; who, from the moment I saw you, have only breathed and sighed for you!"

"Well, now, let us see what you would do to prove this love of which you speak."

"I am all attention, madame," said he.

Milady remained thoughtful and undecided for a moment.

"I have an enemy," said she.

"You, madame!" said D'Artagnan, affecting surprise; "is that possible?"

"An enemy, who has insulted me so cruelly, that between him and me it is war to the death. May I reckon on you as an auxiliary?"

D'Artagnan at once perceived what the vindictive creature was coming to.

"You may, madame," said he, with emphasis. "My arm and my life are yours, as my love is."

"Then," said milady, "since you are as generous as you are loving—" She stopped.

"Well?" demanded D'Artagnan.

"Then you would employ on my account your arm, which has already acquired so much renown?

"Instantly!"

"But on my part," said milady, "how should I repay such a service? I know what lovers are; they are men who do nothing for nothing."

"You know the only reply that I desire," said D'Artagnan.

And he drew nearer to her.

She did not retreat.

"Interested man!" cried she, smiling.

"Ah!" cried D'Artagnan, really carried away by the passion this woman had the power to kindle in him. "Ah! that is because my happiness appears so impossible to me; and I have such fear that it should fly away from me like a dream, that I pant to make a reality of it."

"Well! merit this pretended happiness, then!"

"Only name to me the base man that has brought tears into your beautiful eyes!"

"You know him."

"It is surely not one of my friends?" replied D'Artagnan, affecting hesitation, in order to make her believe him ignorant.

"If it were one of your friends, you would hesitate then?" cried milady; and a threatening glance darted from her eyes.

"Not if it were my own brother!" cried D'Artagnan, as if carried away by his enthusiasm.

And he folded her in his arms. She made no effort to remove her lips from his kisses, only did not respond to them. Her lips were cold; it appeared to D'Artagnan that he had embraced a statue.

"His name is—" said she.

"De Wardes; I know it," cried D'Artagnan.

"And how do you know it?" asked milady, seizing both his hands, and endeavouring to read with her eyes to the bottom of his heart.

D'Artagnan felt he had allowed himself to be carried away, and that he had committed an error.

"Tell me! tell me, I say," repeated milady, "how do you know it?"

"I know it, because yesterday M. de Wardes, in a salon where I was, showed a ring which he said he had of you."

"Miserable scoundrel!" cried milady.

"Well, I will avenge you of this 'miserable scoundrel,'" replied D'Artagnan.

"Thanks! my brave friend!" cried milady; "and when shall I be avenged?"

"You would not, then, prefer a means," resumed D'Artagnan, "which would equally avenge you, whilst rendering combat useless?"

"Really," said she, "I believe you now begin to hesitate."

"No, I do not hesitate; but I really pity this poor Count de Wardes, since you have ceased to love him."

"Who told you that I have loved him?" asked milady sharply.

"Because I alone know—"

"What?"

"That he is far from being, or rather having been, so guilty towards you as he appears to be."

"Indeed!" said milady, in an anxious tone; "explain yourself."

And she looked at D'Artagnan.

"Yes; I am a man of honour," said D'Artagnan, determined to come to an end, "and since your love is mine, and I am satisfied I possess it—for I do possess it, do I not?"

"Entirely; go on."

"Well, I feel as if transformed—a confession weighs on my mind."

"A confession!"

"If I had the least doubt of your love, I would not make it; but you love me, do you not?"

"Without doubt, I do."

"Then if, through excess of love, I have rendered myself culpable towards you, you will pardon me?"

"Perhaps.".

D'Artagnan assumed his most winning smile, but it had no effect; he had alarmed milady, and she involuntarily turned from him.

"This confession," said she, growing paler and paler, "what is this confession!"

"You gave De Wardes a meeting on Thursday last, in this very room, did you not?"

"Who—I? No, certainly not!" said milady, in a tone of voice so firm, and with a countenance so unchanged, that if D'Artagnan had not been in such perfect possession of the fact, he would have doubted.

"Do not say that which is not true, my angel," said D'Artagnan, smiling; "that would be useless."

"What do you mean? Speak! you terrify me to death."

"Be satisfied; you are not guilty towards me—I have already pardoned you."

"What next? what next?"

"De Wardes cannot boast of anything."

"How is that? You told me yourself that that ring—"

"That ring I have! The Count de Wardes of last Thursday and the D'Artagnan of today are the same person!"

The imprudent young man expected a surprise, mixed with shame—a slight storm, which would resolve itself into tears; but he was strangely deceived, and his error was not of long duration.

Pale and trembling, milady repulsed D'Artagnan's attempted embrace by a violent blow on the chest, as she sprang from him.

In his eagerness to detain her, D'Artagnan had grasped her dress; but the frail cambric could not stand against two such strong wills—it was torn from her fair round shoulders, and to his horror and astonishment, D'Artagnan recognized upon one of them, indelibly branded, the mark which is impressed by the ignominious hand of the executioner.

"Great God!" cried D'Artagnan, loosing his hold, and remaining mute, motionless, and frozen.

She turned upon him, no longer like a furious woman, but like a wounded panther.

"Ah! wretch!" cried she, "thou hast basely betrayed me and still more, thou has my secret! Thou shalt die!"

And she flew to a little inlaid casket which stood upon the toilet, opened it with a feverish and trembling hand, drew from it a small poniard with a golden haft and a sharp thin blade, and then threw herself with a bound upon D'Artagnan.

Although the young man was, as we know, brave, he was terrified at that wild countenance, those terribly dilated pupils, those pale cheeks. He drew back to the other side of the room as he would have done from a serpent which was crawling towards him and his sword coming in contact with her nervous hand, he drew it, almost unconsciously, from the scabbard.

But, without taking any heed of the sword, milady endeavoured to get near enough to him to stab him, and did not stop till she felt the sharp point at the throat.

She then endeavoured to seize the sword with her hands, but D'Artagnan kept it free from her grasp and continued to present the point, sometimes at her eyes, sometimes at her breast, whilst he aimed at making his retreat by the door which led to Kitty's apartment.

"Scoundrel! infamous scoundrel!" howled milady.

But D'Artagnan, still keeping on the defensive, drew near to Kitty's door. At the noise they made, she in overturning the furniture in her efforts to get at him, he in screening himself behind the furniture to keep out of her reach, Kitty, in great alarm, opened the door. D'Artagnan, who had constantly manoeuvred to gain this point, was not at more than three paces from it. With one spring he flew from the chamber of milady into that of the maid, and, quick as lightning, he slammed to the door, and placed all his weight against it, whilst Kitty bolted it.

"Quick, Kitty, quick!" said D'Artagnan, in a low voice, as soon as the bolts were fast, "let me get out of the hotel; for if we leave her time to turn round, she will have me killed by the servants!"

At the moment she lost sight of him, milady sank back fainting into her chamber.

XIII

The siege of La Rochelle was one of the great political events of the reign of Louis XIII, and one of the great military enterprises of the Cardinal. Of the cities given by Henry IV to the Huguenots, this town alone remained—the last bulwark of Calvinism, where the ferments of civil revolt and foreign war were constantly mingling. Its port was the last in France open to the English, and by closing it, the Cardinal completed the work of Joan of Arc. He knew that in fighting England he fought Buckingham; that in triumphing over England he triumphed over Buckingham—in short, that in humiliating England in the eyes of Europe he humiliated Buckingham in the eyes of the Queen of France.

Now, one evening, when D'Artagnan, who was in the trenches, was not able to accompany them, Athos, Porthos and Aramis, mounted upon their battle-steeds, enveloped in their war-cloaks, with their hands upon their pistol-butts were returning from a buvette when at about a quarter of a league from the village of Boinar, they fancied they heard the sound of horses approaching them. At the end of an instant, and as the moon broke from behind a cloud, they saw, at a turning of the road, two horsemen, who, on perceiving them, stopped in their turn.

"Beware of what you are about, gentlemen!" said a clear voice, which appeared accustomed to command.

"It is some superior officer, making his night-rounds," said Athos.

"Who are you?" said the same voice in the same commanding tone.

"King's musketeers," said Athos.

"Your name?" said the officer, a part of whose face was covered by his cloak.

"But yourself, monsieur," said Athos, who began to be annoyed by this inquisition, "give me, I beg you, the proof that you have the right to question me."

"Your name?" repeated the cavalier a second time, letting his cloak fall, and leaving his face uncovered.

"Monsieur le Cardinal!" cried the stupefied musketeers.

"Your name?" cried the Cardinal for the third time. "I know you, gentlemen," said the Cardinal, "I know you; I know you are not quite my friends, and I am sorry you are not so; but I know you are brave and loyal gentlemen, and that confidence may be placed in you. Monsieur Athos, do me, then, the honour to accompany me, you and your two friends, and then I shall have an escort to excite envy in his majesty, if we should meet him."

The three musketeers bowed to the necks of their horses.

"Well, upon my honour," said Athos, "your eminence is right in taking us with you; we have seen several ill-looking faces on the road, and we have even had a quarrel at the Red Dovecote with four of those faces."

"A quarrel, and what for, gentlemen?" said the Cardinal; "you know I don't like quarrellers."

"These fellows were drunk," said Athos, "and knowing there was a lady who had arrived at the cabaret this evening, they wanted to force her door."

"And was this lady young and handsome?" asked the Cardinal, with a certain degree of anxiety.

"We did not see her, monsieur," said Athos.

"You did not see her! ah! very well," replied the Cardinal, quickly; "you acted quite rightly in defending the honour of a woman; and as I am going to the Red Dovecote myself, I shall know whether you have told me truth or not."

"Monseigneur," said Athos haughtily, "we are gentlemen, and to save our heads we would not be guilty of a falsehood."

"And now, gentlemen, that's all very well," continued the Cardinal. "I know what I wish to know, follow me."

The three musketeers passed behind his eminence, who again enveloped his face in his cloak, and put his horse in motion, keeping at from eight to ten paces in advance of his companions.

They soon arrived at the silent, solitary auberge; no doubt the host knew what illustrious visitor he expected; and had consequently sent intruders out of the way.

The Cardinal alighted, the three musketeers did so like-

wise; the Cardinal threw the bridle of his horse to his attendant; the three musketeers fastened their horses to the shutter.

The host stood at the door; for him, the Cardinal was only
an officer coming to visit a lady.

"Have you any chamber on the ground floor where these
gentlemen can wait, near a good fire?" said the Cardinal.

The host opened the door of a large room, in which an old
bad stove had just been replaced by a large and excellent
chimney.

"I have this, monsieur," said he.

"That will do," replied the Cardinal, "come in, gentlemen,
and be kind enough to wait for me; I shall not be more than
half an hour."

Whilst thinking and walking, Athos passed and repassed
before the pipe of the stove, broken in half, the other extrem-
ity of which passed into the upper chamber; and every time
he passed, he heard a murmur of words, which at length
fixed his attention. Athos went close to it, and distinguished
some words that appeared to merit so great an interest that
he made a sign to his friends to be silent, remaining himself
bent with his ear directed to the opening of the lower orifice.

"Listen, milady," said the Cardinal, "the affair is important."

"Milady!" murmured Athos.

"I am listening to your eminence with the greatest attention," replied a female voice that made the musketeer start.

"A small vessel, with an English crew, whose captain is
mine, awaits you at the mouth of the Charente, at Forte de
la Pointe; he will set sail tomorrow morning."

"Yes, monseigneur."

"You will go to London" continued the Cardinal; "when
arrived in London you will seek Buckingham."

"I must beg your eminence to observe," said milady, "that
since the affair of the diamond studs, about which the Duke
always suspected me, his grace has been very mistrustful of
me."

"Well, this time," said the Cardinal, "it is not the question
to steal his confidence, but to present yourself frankly and
loyally as a negotiator."

"I will follow your eminence's instructions to the letter."

"You will go to Buckingham on my part, and you will tell
him I am acquainted with all the preparations he has made,

but that they give me no uneasiness, since, at the first step he takes, I will ruin the Queen."

"Will he believe that your eminence is in a position to accomplish the threat you make him?"

"Yes, for I have the proofs."

"But," resumed the lady, "if, in spite of all these reasons, the Duke does not give way, and continues to menace France?"

"If he persists—" His eminence made a pause, and resumed: "if he persists—well, then I shall hope for some one of those events which change the destinies of states."

"Your eminence means, I presume, the knife-stab."

"There will be, in all times and in all countries, particularly if religious divisions exist in those countries, fanatics who ask nothing better than to become martyrs. Aye, and observe, it just recurs to me that the Puritans are furious against Buckingham, and their preachers designate him as the Anti-Christ."

"No doubt," said milady, coolly, "such a fanatic may be ·found."

"Well, such a man would save France."

"He will be found. And now," said milady, "now that I have received the instructions of your eminence as concerns your enemies, monseigneur will permit me to say a few words to him of mine?"

"Who are they?" replied the Duke.

"In the first place, there is a little intriguing woman named Bonacieux."

"She is in the prison of Nantes."

"That is to say, she was there," replied milady; "but the Queen has obtained an order from the King, by means of which she has been conveyed to a convent."

"And what convent?"

"I don't know; the secret has been well kept."

"But I will know!"

"And your eminence will tell me in what convent that woman is?"

"I see nothing inconvenient in that," said the Cardinal.

"Well, now I have an enemy much more to be dreaded by me than this little Madame Bonacieux."

"Who is that?"

"Her lover."

"Ah, ah!" said the Cardinal, "I know whom you mean."

"I mean that wretch D'Artagnan."

"I will send him to the Bastille."

"So far good, monseigneur; but afterwards?"

"When once he is in the Bastille, there is no afterwards!" said the Cardinal, in a low voice.

"Monseigneur," replied milady, "a fair exchange—existence for existence, man for man; give me one, I will give you the other."

"I don't know what you mean, nor do I even desire to know what you mean," replied the Cardinal; "but I wish to please you, and see nothing inconvenient in giving you what you ask for with respect to so mean a creature; the more so as you tell me this paltry D'Artagnan is a libertine, a duellist, and a traitor."

"An infamous scoundrel, monseigneur, an infamous scoundrel."

"Give me a paper, a pen and some ink, then," said the Cardinal.

"Here they are, monseigneur."

There was a moment of silence. Athos, who had not lost a word of the conversation, took his two companions by the hand, and led them to the other end of the room.

"Well," said Porthos, "what do you want, and why do you not let us listen to the end of the conversation?"

"Hush!" said Athos, speaking in a low voice; "we have heard all it was necessary we should hear; besides, I don't prevent you from listening, but I must be gone."

"You must be gone!" said Porthos; "and if the Cardinal asks for you, what answer can we give?"

"You will not wait till he asks; you will speak first, and tell him that I am gone on the look out, because certain expressions of our hosts have given me reason to think the road is not safe; I will say two words about it to the Cardinal's attendant likewise; the rest concerns myself, don't be uneasy about that."

"Be prudent, Athos," said Aramis.

"Be easy on that head," replied Athos, "you know I am cool enough."

Porthos and Aramis resumed their places by the stove pipe.

As to Athos, he went out without any mystery, took his horse which was tied with those of his friends to the fastenings of the shutters, in four words convinced the attendant of the necessity of a vanguard for their return, carefully examined the priming of his pistols, drew his sword and took the road to the camp.

As Athos had foreseen, it was not long before the Cardinal came down; he opened the door of the room in which the musketeers were, and found Porthos playing an earnest game at dice with Aramis. He cast a rapid glance round the room, and perceived that one of his men was missing.

"What became of M. Athos?" asked he.

"Monseigneur," replied Porthos, "he is gone as a scout, upon some words of our host, which made him believe the road was not safe."

"Well, now will you return with me?"

"Well are at your eminence's orders."

"To horse, then, gentlemen; for it is getting late."

Let us leave him to follow the road to the camp protected by his attendant and the two musketeers, and return to Athos.

For some distance he maintained the pace at which he started, but when out of sight, he turned his horse to the right, made a circuit, and came back within twenty paces of a high hedge, to watch the passage of the little troop; having recognized the laced hats of his companions and the golden fringe of the Cardinal's cloak, he waited till the horsemen had turned the angle of the road, and having lost sight of them, he returned at a gallop to the auberge, which was opened to him without hesitation.

The host recognised him.

"My officer," said Athos, "has forgotten to give a piece of very important information to the lady, and has sent me back to repair his forgetfulness."

"Go up," said the host, "she is still in her chamber."

Athos availed himself of the permission, ascended the stairs with his lightest step, gained the landing, and through the open door perceived milady putting on her hat.

He went straight into the chamber and closed the door after him.

At the noise he made in bolting in, milady turned round.

Athos was standing before the door, enveloped in his cloak, with his hat pulled down over his eyes.

"Who are you? and what do you want?" cried she.

"Do you know me, madame?" said he.

Milady made one step forward, and then drew back, as if she had seen a serpent.

"The Count de la Fère!" murmured milady, becoming exceedingly pale, and drawing back till the wall prevented her going any further.

"Yes, milady," replied Athos. "Sit down, madame, and let us talk."

Milady, under the influence of inexpressible terror, sat down without uttering a word.

"You certainly are a demon sent upon the earth!" said Athos. "Your power is great, I know; but you also know that with the help of God men have often conquered the most terrible demons."

Milady arose as if moved by a powerful spring, and her eyes flashed lightning. Athos remained sitting.

"You believed me to be dead, did you not, as I believed you to be? and the name of Athos as well concealed the Count de la Fère, as the name of milady Clarik concealed Anne de Beuil! Was it not so you were called when your honoured brother married us?"

"But," said milady, in a hollow, faint voice, "what brings you back to me? and what do you want with me?"

"I wish to tell you, that whilst remaining invisible to your eyes, I have not lost sight of you."

"You know what I have done and been?"

"I can relate to you, day by day, your actions, from your entrance into the service of the Cardinal to this evening."

Milady was livid.

"You must be Satan!" cried she.

"Perhaps," said Athos, "but, at all events, listen to this. Assassinate the Duke of Buckingham, or cause him to be assassinated, I care very little about that! But do not touch with the tip of your finger a single hair of D'Artagnan, who is a faithful friend, whom I love and defend, or, I swear to you by the head of my father, the crime which you shall have endeavoured to commit, or shall have committed, shall be the last."

"M. D'Artagnan has cruelly insulted me," said milady, in a hollow tone; "M. D'Artagnan shall die!"

"Indeed! is it possible to insult you, madame?" said Athos, laughing.

"He shall die!" replied milady.

Athos arose, reached his hand to his belt, drew forth a pistol, and cocked it.

Milady, pale as a corpse, endeavoured to cry out; but her swollen tongue could not utter more than a hoarse sound.

Athos slowly raised his pistol, stretched out his arm, so that the weapon almost touched milady's forehead, and then in a voice the more terrible from having the supreme calmness of a fixed resolution:

"Madame," said he, "you will this instant deliver to me the paper the Cardinal signed; or, upon my soul, I will blow your brains out."

With another man, milady might have preserved some doubt; but she knew Athos; nevertheless, she remained motionless.

"You have one second to decide," said he.

Milady saw by the contraction of his countenance that the trigger was about to be pulled; she reached her hand quickly to her bosom, drew out a paper, and held it towards Athos.

"Take it," said she, "and be accursed!"

Athos took the paper, returned the pistol to his belt, approached the lamp, to be assured that it was the paper, unfolded it and read:

> It is by my order, and for the good of the state, that the bearer of this has done what he has done.
> August 5th, 1628.
> Richelieu

"And now," said Athos, resuming his cloak, and putting on his hat, "now that I have drawn your teeth, viper, bite if you can."

And he left the chamber without once looking behind him.

At the door he found the two men, and the spare horse which they held.

"Gentlemen," said he, "monseigneur's order is, you know, to conduct that woman, without losing time, to the fort of La Pointe, and never to leave her till she is on board."

As these orders agreed effectively with the order they had received, they bowed their heads in a sign of assent.

After breakfast, it was agreed that the musketeers should meet again in the evening at Athos's lodgings, and would there terminate the affair.

In the evening, at the appointed hour, the four friends met; there only remained one thing to be decided upon:

What they should write to milady's brother.

D'Artagnan and Athos looked at each other for some time in silence.

"Well, this is what you have to say," said D'Artagnan:

" 'Milord, your sister-in-law is an infamous woman, who has wished you to be killed, that she might inherit your wealth. But she could not marry your brother, being already married in France, and having been—' " D'Artagnan stopped, as if seeking for the word, and looking at Athos.

"Repudiated by her husband."

"Because she had been branded," continued D'Artagnan.

"And she was previously married?" asked Aramis.

"Yes."

"And her husband found out that she had a fleur-de-lis on her shoulder?" cried Porthos.

"And who has seen this fleur-de-lis?" said Aramis.

"D'Artagnan and I, or rather, to observe the chronological order, I and D'Artagnan," replied Athos.

"And does this husband of this frightful creature still live?" said Aramis.

"I am he."

There was a moment of cold silence, during which every one was affected, according to his nature.

"This time," said Athos, first breaking the silence, "D'Artagnan has given us an excellent plan, and the letter must be written at once."

Aramis accordingly took the pen, reflecting for a few moments, wrote eight or ten lines, in a charming, little female hand, and then, with a voice soft and slow, as if each word had been scrupulously weighed, he read the following:

Milord,

The person who writes these few lines had the honour of crossing swords with you in the little enclosure of the Rue d'Enfer. As you have several times since declared yourself the friend of that person, he thinks it his duty to respond to that friendship by sending you important advice. Twice you have nearly been the victim of a near-relation whom you believe to be your heir, because you are ignorant that before she contracted a marriage in England, she was already married in France. But the third time, which is this, you may succumb. Your relation left La Rochelle for England during the night. Watch her arrival, for she has great and terrible projects. If you require to know positively what she is capable of, read the past history upon her left shoulder.

"Well, now that will do wonderfully well," said Athos; "really, my dear Aramis, you have the pen of a secretary of state."

Planchet was sent for, and instructions were given him; the matter had been named to him by D'Artagnan, who had, in the first place, pointed out the money to him, then the glory; and then the danger.

"I will carry the letter in the lining of my coat," said Planchet; "and if I am taken I will swallow it."

"Well, but then you will not be able to fulfil your commission," said D'Artagnan.

"You will give me a copy of it this evening, which I shall know by heart before the morning."

D'Artagnan looked at his friends, as if to say, "Well, what did I promise you?"

"Now," continued he, addressing Planchet, "you have eight days to get an interview with Lord de Winter, you have eight days to return in, in all sixteen days; if, on the sixteenth day after your departure, at eight o'clock in the evening, you are not here, no money, even if it be but five minutes past eight—"

"Then, monsieur," said Planchet, "you must buy me a watch."

"Take this," said Athos, with his usual careless generosity, giving him his own, "and be a good lad."

It was determined that Planchet should set out the next day, at eight o'clock in the morning, in order, as he had said, that he might, during the night, learn the letter by heart. He gained just twelve hours by this engagement; he was to be back on the sixteenth day, by eight o'clock in the evening.

In the morning, as he was mounting on horseback, D'Artagnan, who felt at the bottom of his heart a partiality for the Duke, took Planchet aside.

"Listen," said he to him; "when you have given the letter to Lord de Winter, and he has read it, you will further say to him, 'Watch over his grace Lord Buckingham, for they wish to assassinate him.'"

"Be satisfied, monsieur," said Planchet, "you shall see whether confidence can be placed in me or not."

And, mounted on an excellent horse, which he was to leave at the end of twenty leagues, to take the post, Planchet set off at a gallop.

The days of expectation are long, and D'Artagnan in particular, would have wagered that the days were forty-four hours long.

On the sixteenth day, in particular, these signs were so visible in D'Artagnan and his two friends, that they could not remain quiet in one place, and they wandered about, like ghosts, on the road by which Planchet was expected.

"Really," said Athos, "you are not men, but children, to let a woman terrify you so! And what does it amount to, after all? To be imprisoned. Well, but we should be taken out of prison; Madame Bonacieux got out. Wait quietly, then; in two hours, in four, in six hours at latest, Planchet will be here: he promised to be here, and I have very great faith in Planchet's promises, I think him a very good lad."

"But if he does not come?" said D'Artagnan.

"Well, if he does not come, it will be because he has been delayed, that's all. Eh! gentlemen, let us reckon upon accidents! Life is a chaplet of little miseries, which the philosopher unstrings with a smile."

"That's all very well," replied D'Artagnan, "but I am tired of fearing, when I open a fresh bottle, that the wine may come from her ladyship's cellar."

The day, however, passed away, and the evening came on slowly, but it did come; the buvettes were filled with drinkers. They were playing together, as usual, when seven o'clock struck; the patrols were heard passing to double the posts; at half-past seven the retreat was sounded.

"We are lost," said D'Artagnan in Athos's ear.

But, all at once, a shadow appeared in the darkness, the outline of which was familiar to D'Artagnan.

"Monsieur, I have brought your cloak; it is chilly this evening."

"Planchet!" cried D'Artagnan, beside himself with joy.

"Well, yes, Planchet, to be sure," said Athos, "what is there so astonishing in that? He promised to be back by eight o'clock, and eight is just now striking."

At the same time D'Artagnan felt that Planchet slipped a note into his hand.

"I have a note," said he to Athos and his friends.

"That's well," said Athos, "let us go home and read it."

It contained half a line in a hand perfectly British, and of a conciseness as perfectly Spartan: "Thank you, be easy."

"Which means what?"

"Thank you, be easy," said D'Artagnan.

Athos took the letter from the hands of D'Artagnan, drew near to the lamp, set fire to it, and did not leave hold of it till it was reduced to ashes.

Then, calling Planchet,—

"Now, my lad," said he, "you may claim your money. Go to bed, Planchet, and sleep soundly."

"Ma foi, monsieur! that will be the first time I have done so these sixteen days!"

"Or I either!" said D'Artagnan.

XIV

Twelve days after leaving the Charente, pale with fatigue and vexation, milady continued her voyage, and on the very day that Planchet embarked at Portsmouth for France, the messenger of his eminence entered the port in triumph.

All the city was agitated by an extraordinary movement—four large vessels, recently built, had just been launched. Standing on the jetty, his clothes richly laced with gold, his hat ornamented with a white feather which drooped upon his shoulder, Buckingham was seen surrounded by a staff almost as brilliant as himself.

They entered the road, but as they drew near, in order to cast anchor, a little cutter, formidably armed, approached the merchant vessel, in appearance a guard-coast, and dropping its boat into the sea, the latter directed its course to the ladder. This boat contained an officer, a mate, and eight rowers—the officer alone got on board, where he was received with all the deference inspired by the uniform.

The officer conversed a few instants with the captain, and, upon the order of the merchant-captain, the whole crew of the vessel, both passengers and sailors, were called upon deck. Then the officer began to pass in review all the persons, one after the other, and stopping when he came to milady, surveyed her very closely, but without addressing a single word to her.

Then the vessel resumed its course, still escorted by the little cutter, which sailed side by side with it, menacing it with the mouths of its six cannon.

When they entered the port, it was already night. Milady, that woman so courageous and firm, shivered in spite of herself.

The officer desired to have milady's packages pointed out to him, and ordered them to be placed in the boat; when this operation was completed, he invited her to descend by offering her his hand.

Milady looked at this man, and hesitated.

"Who are you, sir," asked she, "who have the kindness to occupy yourself so particularly on my account?"

"You may perceive, madame, by my uniform, that I am an officer in the English navy," replied the young man.

"But is it the custom for the officers in the English navy to place themselves at the service of their female compatriots, when they land in a port of Great Britain, and carry their gallantry so far as to conduct them ashore?"

"Yes, milady, it is the custom, not from gallantry but prudence, that in time of war, foreigners are conducted to particular hotels, in order that they may remain under the surveillance of the government, until perfect information be obtained relative to them."

These words were pronounced with the most exact politeness, and the most perfect calmness. Nevertheless, they had not the power of convincing milady.

"But I am not a foreigner, sir," said she with an accent as pure as ever was heard between Portsmouth and Manchester; "my name is Lady Clarik, and this measure . . ."

"This measure is general, madame; and you will endeavour in vain to evade it."

"I will follow you then, sir."

And accepting the hand of the officer, she commenced the descent of the ladder, at the foot of which the boat awaited. A large cloak was spread at the stern; the officer requested her to sit upon this cloak, and placed himself beside her.

"Row on!" said he to the sailors.

At the expiration of five minutes, they gained the land.

The officer sprang out of the boat, and offered his hand to milady. A carriage was in waiting.

"Is this carriage for us?" asked milady.

"Yes, madame," replied the officer.

"The hotel, then, is at some distance?"

"At the other end of the town."

"Very well," said milady; and she got resolutely into the carriage.

Immediately, without any order being given, or his place of destination indicated, the coachman set off at a rapid pace, and plunged into the streets of the town.

At length, after a journey of near an hour, the carriage stopped before an iron gate, which enclosed an avenue leading to a château severe in form, massive and isolated. Then, as the wheels rolled over a fine gravel, milady could hear a vast roaring; which she at once recognized as the noise of the sea, dashing against some steep coast.

The carriage passed under two arched gateways, and at length stopped in a large, dark, square court; almost immediately, the door of the carriage was opened, the young man sprang lightly out and presented his hand to milady, who leant upon it, and in her turn alighted with tolerable calmness.

"Still, then, I am a prisoner," said milady, looking around her, and bringing back her eyes with a most gracious smile to the young officer; "but I feel assured it will not be for long," added she; "my own conscience and your politeness, sir, are the guarantees of that."

The officer then, with the same calm politeness, invited the lady to enter the house. She, with a still smiling countenance, took his arm, and passed with him under a low arched door, which, by a vaulted passage, lighted only at the far end, led to a stone staircase, turning round an angle of stone; they then came to a massive door, which, after the introduction of a key into the lock, by the young officer, turned heavily upon its hinges, and disclosed the chamber destined for milady. It was a chamber whose furniture was at once proper for a prisoner or a free man; and yet, bars at the windows and outside bolts at the door decided the question in favour of the prison.

In an instant all the strength of mind of this creature, though drawn from the most vigorous sources, abandoned her; she sank into a large chair, with her arms crossed, her head hanging down, and expecting every instant to see a judge enter to interrogate her.

But no one entered except two marines, who brought in

her trunks and packages, deposited them in a corner of the room, and retired without speaking.

The officer presiding over all these details with the same calmness milady had observed in him, never pronouncing a word, and making himself obeyed by a gesture of his hands or a sound of his whistle.

At length milady could hold out no longer; she broke the silence:

"In the name of Heaven, sir!" cried she, "what does all this that is passing mean? Where am I, and why am I here? If I am free, why these bars and these doors?"

"You are here in the apartment destined for you, madam. I received orders to go and take charge of you at sea, and to conduct you to this château; this order, I believe, I have accomplished with all the exactness of a soldier, but also with the courtesy of a gentleman. There terminates, at least to the present moment, the duty I had to fulfil towards you, the rest concerns another person."

"And who is that other person?" asked milady, warmly; "can you tell me his name?"

At the moment a great jingling of spurs was heard upon the stairs; some voices passed, and faded away, and the sound of one footstep approached the door.

"That person is here, madam," said the officer, leaving the entrance open, and drawing himself up in an attitude of respect.

At the same time the door opened; a man appeared in the opening. He was without a hat, wore a sword, and carried a handkerchief in his hand.

Milady thought she recognised this shadow in the shade; she supported herself with one hand upon the arm of the chair, and advanced her head as if to meet a certainty.

The stranger advanced slowly, and as he advanced, after entering into the circle of light projected by the lamp, milady involuntarily drew back.

Then, when she had no longer any doubt:

"What! my brother," cried she, in a state of stupor, "is it you?"

"Yes, fair lady!" replied Lord de Winter, making a bow, half courteous, half ironical—"it is I, myself."

"But this château, then?"

"Is mine."

"I am your prisoner, then?"

"Nearly so."

"Let us chat, brother," said she, with a kind of cheerfulness.

"You were, then, determined to come to England again?" said Lord de Winter.

Milady replied to this question with another question.

"Before everything," said she, "how happens you to have watched me so closely, as to be beforehand aware, not only of my arrival, but still more, of the day, the hour, and the port, at which I should arrive?"

Lord de Winter adopted the same tactics as milady, thinking that as his sister-in-law employed them, they must be the best.

"But tell me, my dear sister," replied he, "what are you come to do in England?"

"Come for? why, to see you," replied milady; without knowing how much she aggravated, by this reply, the suspicions, which D'Artagnan's letter had given birth to in the mind of her brother-in-law, and only desiring to gain the good will of her auditor by a falsehood.

"Humph! to see me?" said De Winter, as if doubtingly.

"To be sure, to see you. What is there astonishing in that?"

"So it was for my sake alone you have taken the trouble to cross the channel?"

"For your sake only."

"The deuce! what tenderness, my sister!"

"Why, am I not your nearest relation?" demanded milady with a tone of the most touching ingenuousness.

"And my only heir, are you not?" said Lord de Winter in his turn, fixing his eyes on those of milady.

Whatever command she had over herself, milady could not help starting, and as, in pronouncing the last words, Lord de Winter placed his hand upon the arm of his sister, this start did not escape him.

"I do not comprehend, my lord," said she, to gain time and make her adversary speak out. "What do you mean to say? Is there any secret meaning concealed beneath your words?"

"Oh! good lord! no," said Lord de Winter, "you wish to see me, and you come to England. What is there more astonishing in all that I have said to you, than in that which you have told me?"

"No, all that I think astonishing is that you should be aware of my coming."

"And yet that is the most simple thing in the world, my dear sister; have you not observed that the captain of your little vessel, on entering the road, sent forward, to obtain permission to enter the port, a little boat bearing his log-book and the register of his crew? I am commandant of the port, they brought me that book. I recognised your name in it. I sent my cutter to meet you. You know the rest."

Milady comprehended that Lord de Winter lied, and was only the more alarmed.

"Brother," continued she, "was not that Milord Buckingham whom I saw on the jetty, this evening, as we entered the port?"

"Ah! I can understand how the sight of him struck you," replied Lord de Winter: "you came from a country where he must be very much talked of, and I know that his armaments against France greatly engage the attention of your friend the Cardinal."

"My friend the Cardinal!" cried milady, seeing that, upon this point as upon the other, Lord de Winter seemed perfectly well informed.

"Is he not your friend?" replied the baron, negligently; "but we will return to my lord duke presently, let us not depart from the sentimental turn our conversation had taken: you came, you say, to see me?"

"Yes."

"Well! I reply to you that you shall be attended to the height of your wishes, and that we shall see each other every day."

"Am I then to remain here eternally?" demanded milady with terror.

"Do you find yourself ill lodged, sister? Ask for anything you want, and I will hasten to have you furnished with it."

"But I have neither my women, nor my servants."

"You shall have all that, madame. Tell me on what footing your household was established by your first husband, and although I am only your brother-in-law, I will arrange it upon a similar one."

"My first husband!" cried milady, looking at Lord de Winter, with eyes almost starting from their sockets.

"Yes, your French husband; I don't speak of my brother.

If you have forgotten, as he is still living, I can write to him, and he will send me information on that subject."

A cold sweat broke from the brow of milady.

"You are joking!" said she, in a hollow, broken voice.

"Do I look as if I were?" asked the baron, rising and going a step backward.

"In truth, sir," said milady, "you must be either drunk or mad; leave the room, sir, and send me a woman."

"Women are very indiscreet, sister! cannot I serve you as a waiting maid? by that means, all our secrets would be kept in the family."

"Insolent wretch!" cried milady, and, as if acted upon by a spring, she rushed towards the baron, who awaited her attack with his arms crossed, but one hand upon the hilt of his sword.

"Come! come!" said he, "I know you are accustomed to assassinate people, but I shall defend myself, I give you notice, even against you."

"No doubt you would!" said she; "you have all the appearance of being coward enough to lift your hand against a woman."

"Perhaps I have, and I have an excuse, for mine would not be the first man's hand that has been placed upon you, I imagine."

And the baron pointed with a slow and accusing gesture to the left shoulder of milady, which he almost touched with his finger.

Milady uttered a deep inward shriek, and retreated to a corner of the room, like a panther which draws back to take its spring.

"Yes, I can very well understand that after having inherited the fortune of my brother, it would be very agreeable to you to be my heir likewise; but know, beforehand, if you kill me, or cause me to be killed, my precautions are taken: not a penny of what I possess will pass into your hands."

Milady listened with an attention that dilated her inflamed eyes.

"Yes, at present," continued Lord de Winter, "you will remain in this castle. Ah! I see your features are resuming their calmness, your countenance is recovering its assurance: fifteen days, twenty days, say you, bah! Before fifteen days are gone by, you say to yourself, I shall be away from here! Well, try!"

Milady, finding her thoughts betrayed, dug her nails into her flesh, to subdue every emotion that might give to her physiognomy any expression beyond that of pain.

Lord de Winter continued:

"The officer who commands here in my absence you have already seen. He knows how to obey an order. You have already tried the power of your seductions upon many men, and, unfortunately, you have always succeeded; but I give you leave to try them upon this one: pardieu! if you succeed with him, I pronounce you the demon himself."

He went towards the door and opened it hastily.

"Call Master Felton," said he.

There followed between these two personages a strange silence, during which the sound of a slow and regular step was heard approaching; shortly a human form appeared in the shade of the corridor, and the young lieutenant, with whom we are already acquainted, stopped at the door, to receive the orders of the baron.

"Come in, my dear John," said Lord de Winter, "come in, and shut the door."

The young officer entered.

"Now," said the baron, "look at this woman: she is young, she is beautiful, she possesses all earthly seductions. Well she is a monster, who, at twenty-five years of age, has been guilty of as many crimes as you could read of in a year in the archives of our tribunals; she will endeavour to seduce you, perhaps she will endeavour to kill you. I have extricated you from misery, Felton, I have caused you to be named lieutenant. I once saved your life, you know on what occasion; I hold this serpent in my power; well, I call upon you, and say to you: Friend Felton, John, my child, guard me, and more particularly guard yourself against this woman; swear by your hopes of salvation to keep her safely for the chastisement she has merited. John Felton, I put faith in thy loyalty!"

"My lord," said the young officer, summoning to his mild countenance all the hatred he could find in his heart; "my lord, I swear all shall be done as you desire."

Milady received this look like a resigned victim: it was impossible to imagine a more submissive or a more mild expression than that which prevailed on her beautiful countenance.

"She is not to leave this chamber, understand, John; she is not to correspond with anyone, she is to speak to no one but you—if you will do her the honour to address a word to her."

"That is quite sufficient, my lord! I have sworn."

"And now, madame, try to make your peace with God, for you are adjudged by men!"

Milady let her head sink, as if crushed by this sentence, Lord de Winter went out, making a sign to Felton, who followed him, shutting the door after him.

XV

Milady dreamed that she at length had D'Artagnan in her power, that she was present at his execution.

In the morning, when they entered her chamber, she was still in bed. Felton remained in the corridor; he brought with him a woman. This woman entered, approaching milady's bed.

Milady was habitually pale; her complexion might therefore deceive a person who saw her for the first time.

"I am in a fever," said she; "I have not slept a single instant during all this long night—I am in frightful pain."

"Would you like to have a physician sent for?" said the woman.

"A physician!" said she: "what would be the good of that?"

"If you are really in pain," said Felton, "a physician shall be sent for; and if you deceive us, well! why it will be the worse for you, but at least we shall not have to reproach ourselves with anything."

Milady made no reply, but turning her beautiful head round upon her pillow, she burst into tears, and uttered heartbreaking sobs.

Felton surveyed her for an instant, then, seeing that the crisis threatened to be prolonged, he went out; the woman followed him.

"I fancy I begin to see my way," murmured milady, with a

savage joy, burying herself under the clothes to conceal from anybody who might be watching her, this burst of inward satisfaction.

Two hours passed away.

In the morning, when the woman and Felton came, they had brought her breakfast; now she thought they could not be long before they came to clear the table, and that Felton would then come back.

Milady was not deceived: Felton reappeared, and without observing whether she had or had not touched her repast, he made a sign that the table should be carried out of the room.

Felton remained behind: he held a book in his hand.

Milady, reclining in a fauteuil, near the chimney, beautiful, pale and resigned, looked like a holy virgin awaiting martyrdom.

Felton approached her, and said:

"Lord de Winter, who is a Catholic, as well as yourself, madame, thinking that the privation of the rites and ceremonies of your church might be painful to you, has consented that you should read every day the ordinary of your mass, and here is a book which contains the ritual of it."

At the manner in which Felton pronounced the two words "your mass", at the disdainful smile with which he accompanied them, milady raised her head, and looked more attentively at the officer.

Then, by that plain arrangement of the hair, by that costume of extreme simplicity, she recognised one of those dark Puritans she had so often met with.

She then had one of those sudden inspirations which people of genius alone have in great crisis.

"I!" said she, with an accent of disdain in unison with that which she had remarked in the voice of the young officer, "I sir; my mass! Lord de Winter, the corrupted Catholic knows very well that I am not of his religion, and this is a snare he wishes to lay for me!"

"And of what religion are you, then, madame?" asked Felton, with an astonishment which he could not entirely conceal.

"I will tell it," cried milady, with a feigned exultation, "on the day when I shall have suffered sufficiently for my faith."

The look of Felton revealed to milady the full extent of the space she had opened for herself by this single word.

"I am in the hands of mine enemies," confided she, with

that tone of enthusiasm which she knew was familiar to the Puritans: "well, let my God save me, or let me perish for my God! And as to this book," added she, pointing the ritual with her finger, but without touching it, as if she must be contaminated by the touch, "you may carry it back and make use of it yourself; for, doubtless, you are doubly the accomplice of Lord de Winter; the accomplice in his persecutions, the accomplice in his heresies."

Felton made no reply, took the book with the same appearance of repugnance which he had before manifested, and retired pensively.

Silence was re-established—hours passed away; milady's supper was brought in, and she was found deeply engaged in saying her prayers aloud; prayers which she had learnt of an old servant of her second husband's, a most austere Puritan. She appeared to be in ecstasy, and did not pay the least attention to what was going on around her. Felton made a sign that she would not be disturbed; and when all was arranged, he went out quietly with the soldiers.

Milady knew she might be watched, so she continued the prayers to the end, and it appeared to her that the soldier who was on duty at the door did not march with the same step, and seemed to listen.

For the moment she required no more; she arose, placed herself at table, ate but little, and drank only water. An hour after, her table was cleared; but milady remarked that this time Felton did not accompany the soldiers.

He feared, then, to see her too often.

She allowed, therefore, half an hour to pass away; and as at that moment all was silence in the old castle, she began to sing:

> For all my tears and all my cares,
> My exile and my chains,
> I have my youth, I have my prayers,
>   And God who counts my pains.

This verse, into which the terrible enchantress threw her whole soul, completed the trouble which had seized the heart of the young officer; he opened the door quickly, and milady saw him appear, pale as usual, but with his eyes inflamed and almost wild.

"Why do you sing thus, and with such a voice?" said he.

"I crave your pardon, sir," said milady, with mildness; "I forgot that my songs are out of place in this mansion. I have perhaps offended you in your religious opinions; but it was without wishing to do so, I assure you."

Milady was so beautiful at this moment—the religious ecstasy in which she appeared to be plunged gave such an expression to her countenance, that Felton was dazzled.

"Yes, yes," said he, "you disturb—you agitate the people who inhabit the castle."

"I will be silent then," said milady, casting down her eyes with all the sweetness she could give to her voice.

"No, no, madame," said Felton; "only do not sing so loud, particularly at night."

And at these words, Felton, feeling that he could not long maintain his severity towards his prisoner, rushed out of the room.

The next day, when Felton entered milady's apartment, he found her standing, mounted upon a chair, holding in her hands a cord made by means of torn cambric handkerchiefs, twisted into a kind of rope one with another, and tied at the ends; at the noise Felton made in entering, milady leaped lightly to the ground, and endeavoured to conceal behind her the improvised cord she held in her hand.

He advanced slowly towards milady, who had sat down, and taking an end of the murderous rope, which by mistake or else by design, she allowed to appear—

"What is this, madame?" he asked, coldly.

"Nothing," said milady, smiling with that painful expression which she knew so well how to give to her smile.

Felton turned his eyes towards the part of the wall of the apartment before which he had found milady standing on the chair in which she was now seated, and over her head he perceived a gilt-headed screw, fixed in the wall, for the purpose of hanging up clothes or arms.

He started, and the prisoner saw that start; for, though her eyes were cast down, nothing escaped her.

"What were you doing, standing in that chair?" asked he.

"Do not question me," said the prisoner, "you know that we true Christians are forbidden to speak falsely."

"Well, then," said Felton, "I will tell you what you were doing, or rather what you were going to do; you were going to complete the fatal work you cherish in your mind; remember, madame, if our God forbids us to speak falsely, he much more severely forbids us to commit suicide."

"When God sees one of his creatures persecuted unjustly, placed between suicide and dishonour, believe me, sir," replied milady in a tone of deep conviction, "God pardons suicide; for then, suicide becomes martyrdom."

"What have I then done to you," said Felton, much agitated, "that you should load me with such a responsibility before God and before men?"

"So," cried milady, as if she could not resist giving utterance to a holy indignation, "you ask but one thing—and that is that you may not be inculpated, annoyed, by my death!"

Milady saw the trouble, she felt by intuition the flame of the opposing passions which burned with the blood in the veins of the young fanatic; she rose, inspired like a Christian virgin, her arms extended, her hair dishevelled, holding with one hand her robe modestly drawn over her breast, her look illuminated by that fire which had already created such disorder in the veins of the young Puritan, she stepped towards him, crying out with a vehement air, and in her melodious voice, to which, on this occasion, she communicated a terrible energy:

> Let his victim to Baal be sent,
>   To the lions the martyr be thrown,
> Thy God shall teach thee to repent!
>   From th'abyss he'll give ear to my moan.

Felton stood before this strange apparition, like one petrified.

"Who art thou?" cried he, clasping his hands: "Art thou a messenger from God?"

"Do you not know me, Felton? I am neither an angel nor a demon, I am a daughter of earth, I am a sister of thy faith, that is all."

"Yes! yes!" said Felton, "I doubted but now I believe!"

"You believe, and yet you deliver me up to him who fills and defies the world with his heresies and debaucheries, to that infamous Sardanapalus; whom the blind call the Duke of Buckingham, and whom true believers name Antichrist!"

"I deliver you up to Buckingham!"

"They have eyes," cried milady, "and they will not see; they have ears, and they will not hear."

"Yes! Yes!" said Felton, passing his hands over his brow, covered with sweat, as if to remove his last doubt; "yes, I recognise the voice which speaks to me in my dreams; yes, I recognise the features of the angel that appears to me every night, crying to my soul, which cannot sleep: 'Strike, save England, save thyself, for thou wilt die without having disarmed God!'—Speak! Speak!" cried Felton, "I can understand you now."

"Confide my shame to you," cried milady, with the blush of modesty upon her countenance, "for often the crime of one becomes the shame of another; confide my shame to you, a man, and I a woman! Oh!" continued she, placing her hand modestly over her beautiful eyes, "never! never!—I could not!"

"Listen," replied Felton in a low voice; "I have just sent away the sentinel, that I might speak to you without having what I say to you overheard by others. The baron has just related a frightful history to me."

Milady assumed her smile of a resigned victim, and shook her head.

"Either you are a demon," continued Felton, "or the baron, my benefactor, my father, is a monster. Tonight, after twelve, I will come and see and listen to you, and you will convince me."

"No, Felton, my brother, the sacrifice is too great, and I feel what it must cost you. My death will be much more eloquent than my life, and the silence of the corpse will convince you much better than the words of the prisoner."

"Be silent, madame," cried Felton, "and do not speak to me thus; I came to entreat you to promise me upon your honour, to swear to me by what you hold most sacred, that you will make no attempt upon your life."

"I will not promise," said milady, "for no one has more respect for a promise or an oath than I have, and if I make a promise I must keep it."

"Well," said Felton, "only promise till after you have seen me again. If, when you have seen me again, you still persist—well! then you shall be free."

"Well!" said milady, "for your sake I will wait."

At nine o'clock, Lord de Winter made his customary visit, examined the window and the bars, sounded the floor and the walls, looked to the chimney and the doors, without, during this long and minute examination, he or milady pronouncing a single word.

The clock struck twelve, the sentinel was relieved.

This time it was the hour, and from this moment milady waited with impatience.

The new sentinel commenced his walk in the corridor.

At the expiration of ten minutes, Felton came.

Milady was all attention.

"Here is the knife!" said Felton, drawing from his pocket the weapon which, according to his promise, he had brought, but which he hesitated to give to the prisoner.

"Let me see it," said milady.

"For what purpose?"

"Upon my honour I will instantly return it to you; you shall place it on that table, and you may remain between it and me."

Felton held out the weapon to milady, who examined the temper of it attentively, and who tried the point on the tip of her finger.

"Well," said she, returning the knife to the young officer, "this is fine and good steel; you are a faithful friend, Felton."

Felton took back the weapon, and laid it upon the table, as had been agreed.

Milady followed him with her eyes, unable to refrain from a gesture of satisfaction.

"Now," said she, "listen to me."

The recommendation was useless; the young officer stood upright before her, awaiting her word, as if to devour them.

"Felton," said milady, with a solemnity full of melancholy, "if your sister, the daughter of your father, said to you:

"Still young, unfortunately handsome, I was dragged into a snare, I resisted; ambushes and violences were multiplied around me, I resisted; the religion I serve, the God I adore, were blasphemed because I called upon that religion and that God resisted; then outrages were heaped upon me, and as my soul was not subdued, it was determined to defile my body for ever. In short—"

Milady stopped, and a bitter smile passed over her lips.

"In short," said Felton, "in short, what did they do?"

"At length, one evening, my enemy resolved to paralyse the resistance he could not conquer; one evening he mixed a powerful narcotic with my water. Scarcely had I finished my

repast, when I felt myself sink by degrees into a strange stor-
por. Of all that passed in that sleep, or the time which glided
away whilst it lasted, I have no remembrance; the only thing
I recollect is the noise of a door turning on its hinges made
me start; a globe of fire appeared above the glazed opening
of the ceiling, casting a strong light into my chamber, and I
perceived with terror that a man was standing within a few
paces of me. That man was he who had pursued me during a
whole year, who had vowed my dishonour, and who, by the
first words that issued from his mouth, gave me to understand he had accomplished it."

"Infamous villain!" murmured Felton.

"Oh, yes, infamous villain!" cried milady, seeing the interest which the young officer, whose soul seemed to hang on
her lips, took in this strange recital.

"I dragged myself towards the bed, to seek the only defence I had left—my preserver knife—but I could not reach
the bolster; I sank on my knees, my hands clasped round one
of the bed-posts; then I felt that I was lost."

Felton became frightfully pale, and a convulsive tremor
crept through his whole body.

"Tell me who this man was!" cried the young officer.

Milady saw at a single glance all the painful feelings she
inspired in Felton, by dwelling on every detail of her recital.
She continued then, as if she had not heard his exclamation,
or as if she thought the moment was not yet come to reply to
it.

"My first impulse, on coming to myself, was to feel under
my pillow for the knife I had not been able to reach; if it
had not been useful for defence, it might at least serve in ex-
planation. But on taking this knife, Felton, a terrible thing
occurred to me; I have sworn to tell you all, and I will tell
you all; I have promised you the truth—I will tell it, were it
to destroy me."

"The idea came into your mind to avenge yourself on this
man, did it not?" cried Felton.

"Yes," said milady. "The idea was not that of a Christian,
I knew; but, without, that eternal enemy of our souls, that
lion roaring constantly around us, breathed it into my mind.
In short, what shall I say to you, Felton?" continued milady,
in the tone of a woman accusing herself of a crime. "This
idea occurred to me, and did not leave me; it is of this homi-
cidal thought that I now bear the punishment."

"Continue! continue!" said Felton: "I am eager to see you attain your vengeance!"

"Oh! I resolved that it should take place as soon as possible; I had no doubt he would return the following night. When the evening came, I was so weak that at every time that I fainted I thanked God, for I thought I was about to die. In the midst of one of these faintings, I heard the door open; terror called me to myself. He entered the apartment, followed by a man in a mask; he was masked likewise; but I knew his step, I knew his voice."

" 'Executioner,' said he, 'do your duty.' "

"Oh! his name, his name!" cried Felton, "tell it me!"

"Then, in spite of my cries, in spite of my resistance, for I began to comprehend that there was a question of something worse than death, the executioner seized me, threw me on the floor, fastened me with his bonds, and suffocated by sobs, almost without sense, invoking God, who did not listen to me, I uttered all at once a frightful cry of pain and shame; a burning fire, a red hot iron, the iron of the executioner, was imprinted on my shoulder."

Felton uttered a groan.

"Here," said milady, rising with the majesty of a queen—"here, Felton, behold the new martyrdom invented for a pure young girl, the victim of the brutality of a villain."

Milady, with a rapid gesture, opened her robe, tore the cambric that covered her bosom, and red with feigned anger and simulated shame, showed the young man the ineffaceable impression which dishonoured that beautiful shoulder.

"But," cried Felton, "that is a fleur-de-lis which I see there."

"And therein consisted the infamy," replied milady. "The brand of England!—it would be necessary to prove what tribunal had imposed it on me, and I could have made a public appeal to all the tribunals of the kingdom; but the brand of France!—oh, by it, by it, I was really branded indeed!"

This was too much for Felton.

Pale, motionless, overwhelmed by this frightful revelation, dazzled by the superhuman beauty of this woman, who unveiled herself before him with an immodesty which appeared to him sublime, he ended by falling on his knees before her.

"Pardon! pardon!" cried Felton, "oh! pardon!"

Milady read in his eyes, love! love!

"Pardon for what?" asked she.

"Pardon for having joined with your persecutors."

Milady held out her hand to him.

"So beautiful! so young!" cried Felton, covering that hand with his kisses.

Milady let one of those looks fall upon him which make a slave of a king.

Felton was a Puritan; he abandoned the hand of this woman to kiss her feet.

He no longer loved her, he adored her.

"Ah! now," said he, "I have only one thing to ask of you, that is, the name of your true executioner, for, for me there is but one; the other was an instrument, that was all."

"What, brother!" cried milady, "must I name him again, have you not yet divined who he is?"

"What!" cried Felton, "he!—again he!—always he!"

"The true guilty," said milady, "is the ravager of England, the persecutor of true believers, the base ravisher of the honour of so many women, he who, to satisfy a caprice of his corrupt heart, is about to make England shed so much blood, who protects the Protestants today and will betray them to-morrow—"

"Buckingham! it is, then, Buckingham!" cried Felton, in a high state of exasperation.

Milady concealed her face in her hands, as if she could not endure the shame which this name recalled to her.

"But how can Lord de Winter, my protector, my father," asked Felton, "possibly be mixed up in all this?"

"Well, Buckingham heard by some means, no doubt, of my return. He spoke of me to Lord de Winter, already prejudiced against me; and told him that his sister-in-law was a prostitute, a branded woman. The noble and pure voice of my husband was no longer there to defend me. Lord de Winter believed all that was told him. He caused me to be arrested, had me conducted hither, and placed me under your guard. You know the rest. Oh! the scheme is well laid! the plot is clever! my honour will not survive it! You see, then, Felton, I can do nothing but die! Felton, give me that knife!"

And, at these words, as if all her strength was exhausted, milady sank weak and languishing into the arms of the young officer, who, intoxicated with love, anger, and hitherto unknown sensations of delight, received her with transport, pressed her against his heart, all trembling at the breath from the charming mouth, bewildered by the contact with that beautiful bosom.

"No, no," said he, "no, you shall live honoured and pure, you shall live to triumph over your enemies."

Milady put him from her slowly with the hand, whilst drawing him nearer with her look; but Felton, in his turn, embraced her more closely, imploring her like a divinity.

"Oh, death! death!" said she, lowering her voice and her eyelids; "oh, death rather than shame! Felton, my brother, my friend, I conjure you!"

"No," cried Felton, "no, you shall live, and you shall be avenged."

"Felton, I bring misfortune to all who surround me! Felton abandon me! Felton, let me die!"

"Well, then, we will live and die together!" cried he, gluing his lips to those of the prisoner.

Several strokes resounded on the door; this time milady really pushed him away from her.

"Hark!" said she; "we have been overheard; some one is coming! all is over! we are lost!"

"No," said Felton, "it is only the sentinel warning me that they are about to change guard."

"Then run to the door and open it yourself."

Felton obeyed, this woman was now his whole thought, his whole soul.

He found a sergeant commanding a watch patrol.

Felton, quite bewildered, almost mad, stood speechless.

Milady plainly perceived that it was now her turn to come forward; she ran to the table, and seizing the knife which Felton had laid down,—

"And by what right will you prevent me from dying?" said she.

"Great God!" exclaimed Felton, on seeing the knife glitter in her hand.

At that moment a burst of ironical laughter resounded through the corridor. The baron, attracted by the noise, in his robe-de-chambre, his sword under his arm, stood in the doorway.

"Ah! ah!" said he: "here we are, arrived at the last act of the tragedy. You see, Felton, the drama has gone through all the phases I named; but be at ease, no blood will flow."

Milady perceived that all was lost unless she gave Felton an immediate and terrible proof of her courage.

"You are mistaken, my lord, blood will flow; and may that blood fall back on those who cause it to flow."

Felton uttered a cry, and rushed towards her; he was too late; milady had stabbed herself.

But the knife had fortunately, we ought to say skilfully, come in contact with the steel husk, which at that period, like a cuirass, defended the chests of the women; it had glided down it, tearing the robe, and had penetrated slantingly between the flesh and the ribs.

Milady's robe was not the less stained with blood in a second.

Felton snatched away the knife.

"See, my lord," said he, in a deep, gloomy tone, "here is a woman who was under my guard, and who has killed herself."

"Be at ease, Felton," said Lord de Winter, "she is not dead; demons do not die so easily. Be at ease, and go and wait for me in my chamber."

"But, my lord!—"

"Go, sir, I command you."

At this injunction from his superior, Felton obeyed; but, in going out, he put the knife into his bosom.

As to Lord de Winter, he contented himself with calling his woman who waited on milady, and when she was come, he recommended the prisoner, who was still fainting, to her care, and left her alone with her.

But as, all things considered, notwithstanding his suspicions, the wound might be serious, he immediately sent off a man and horse to fetch a doctor.

XVI

As Lord de Winter had thought, milady's wound was not dangerous. There was no longer a doubt that Felton was convinced: Felton was hers.

Towards four o'clock in the morning, the doctor arrived;

but since the time milady had stabbed herself, however short, the wound had closed. The doctor could, therefore, measure neither the direction nor the depth of it; he only satisfied himself that, by milady's pulse, the case was not serious.

Although she had eaten nothing in the morning, the dinner was brought in at its usual time; milady then perceived with terror that the uniform of the soldiers that guarded her was changed.

Then she ventured to ask what had become of Felton.

She was told that he had left the castle an hour before, on horseback. She inquired if the baron was still at the castle. The soldier replied that he was, and that he had given orders to be informed if the prisoner wished to speak to him.

Milady replied that she was too weak at present.

At six o'clock, Lord de Winter came in: he was armed at all points.

A single look at milady informed him of all that was passing in her mind.

"Aye!" said he, "I see; but you shall not kill me today; you have no longer a weapon; and besides, I am on my guard. You began to pervert my poor Felton; he was yielding to your infernal influence; but I will save him,—he will never see you again,—all is over. Get your clothes together, tomorrow you shall go. Tomorrow, by twelve o'clock, I shall have the order for your exile, signed—'Buckingham.' If you speak a single word to anyone before being on shipboard, my sergeant will blow your brains out; he has orders to do so; if, when on board, you speak a single word to anyone before the captain permits you, the captain will have you thrown into the sea,—that is agreed upon."

At these words the baron went out.

The storm came on about ten o'clock; milady felt a consolation in seeing nature partake of the disorder of her heart.

All at once she heard a tap on her window, and by the help of a flash of lightning, she saw the face of a man appear behind the bars. She ran to the window and opened it.

"Felton!" cried she,—"I am saved!"

"Yes!" said Felton; "but be silent! I must have time to file through these bars."

"But what must I do?" asked milady.

"Nothing! only shut the window. Go to bed, or at least lie down in your clothes; as soon as I have done I will knock on one of the panes of glass. But are you strong enough to follow me?"

"Oh! yes!"

"Your wound?"

"Gives me pain, but will not prevent my walking."

"Be ready, then, at the first signal."

At the expiration of an hour, Felton tapped again.

Milady sprang out of bed and opened the window. Two bars removed formed an opening large enough for a man to pass through.

"Are you ready?" asked Felton.

"Yes. Must I take anything with me?"

"Money, if you have any."

"Yes, fortunately, they have left me all I had."

"So much the better, for I have expended all mine in hiring a vessel."

"Here!" said milady, placing a bag full of louis in Felton's hands.

Felton took the bag and threw it to the foot of the wall.

"Now," said he, "will you come?"

"I am ready."

Milady mounted upon a chair, and passed the upper part of her person through the window; she saw the young officer suspended over the abyss by a ladder of ropes. For the first time, an emotion of terror reminded her that she was a woman.

"Have you confidence in me?" said Felton.

"How can you ask me such a question?"

"Put your two hands together. Cross them—that's right!"

Felton tied her two wrists together with a handkerchief, and then over the handkerchief, with a cord.

"Pass your arms round my neck, and fear nothing."

"But I shall make you lose your balance, and we shall both be dashed to pieces."

"Don't be afraid; I am a sailor."

Not a second was to be lost; milady passed her arms round Felton's neck, and let herself slip out of the window. Felton began to descend the ladder slowly, step by step; notwithstanding the weight of their bodies, the blast of the hurricane made them wave in the air.

All at once Felton stopped.

"What is the matter?" asked milady.

"Silence," said Felton. "I hear footsteps."

Both remained suspended, motionless and breathless, within twenty paces of the ground, whilst the patrol passed beneath them, laughing and talking.

This was a terrible moment for the fugitives.

The patrol passed: the noise of their retreating footsteps and the murmur of their voices soon died away.

"Now," said Felton, "we are safe."

Milady breathed a deep sigh and fainted.

Felton continued to descend. At length, arrived at the last step, he hung by his hands and touched the ground. He stooped down, picked up the bag of money, and carried it in his teeth. Then he took milady in his arms and set off briskly in the direction opposite to that which the patrol had taken. He descended across the rocks, and when they arrived on the edge of the sea, whistled.

A similar signal replied to him, and five minutes after, a boat appeared, rowed by four men.

The boat approached as near as it could to the shore, but there was not depth of water enough for it to touch; and Felton walked into the sea up to his middle, being unwilling to trust his precious burden to anybody.

"To the sloop," said Felton, "and row quickly." Whilst the boat was advancing with all the speed its four rowers could give it, Felton untied the cord, and then the handkerchief which bound milady's hands together. When her hands were loosed, he took some sea-water and sprinkled it over her face.

Milady breathed a sigh and opened her eyes.

"Where am I?" said she.

"Saved," replied the young officer.

"Oh! saved!" cried she. "Yes, there are the heavens, here is the sea."

The young man pressed her to his heart.

Milady looked around her, as if in search of something.

"It is there," said Felton, touching the bag of money with his foot.

They drew near to the sloop. A sailor on watch hailed the boat, the boat replied.

"What vessel is that?" asked milady.

"The one I have hired for you."

"Where is it to take me to?"

"Where you please, after you have put me on shore at Portsmouth."

"What are you going to do at Portsmouth?" asked milady.

"To accomplish the orders of Lord de Winter," said Felton, with a gloomy smile. "As he mistrusted me, he determined to guard you himself, and sent me in his place to get Buckingham to sign the order for your transportation."

"But if he mistrusted you, how could he confide such an order to you?"

"How could I be supposed to know what I was the bearer of?"

"That's true! And you are going to Portsmouth!"

"I have no time to lose: tomorrow is the 23rd, and Buckingham sets sail tomorrow with his fleet."

"He sets sail tomorrow! Where for?"

"For La Rochelle."

"He must not sail!" cried milady, forgetting her usual presence of mind.

"Be satisfied," replied Felton: "he will not sail."

Milady started with joy; she could read to the depths of the heart of this young man; the death of Buckingham was there written at full length.

"Silence," said Felton; "we are arrived."

They were, in fact, close to the sloop.

Felton ascended first, and gave his hand to milady, whilst the sailors supported her, for the sea was still much agitated.

"Captain," said Felton, "this is the person of whom I spoke to you, and whom you must convey safe and sound to France."

"For a thousand pistoles," said the captain.

"I have paid you five hundred of them."

"That's correct," said the captain.

"And here are the other five hundred," replied milady placing her hand upon the bag of gold.

"No," said the captain, "I make but one bargain; and I have agreed with this young man that the other five hundred shall not be due to me till we arrive at Boulogne."

"In the meanwhile," said Felton, "convey me to the little bay of—you know it was agreed you should put me in there."

The captain replied by ordering the necessary manoeuvres, and towards seven o'clock in the morning the little vessel cast anchor in the bay that had been named.

It was agreed that milady should wait for Felton till ten

o'clock; if he did not return by ten o'clock, she was to sail without him.

In that case, and supposing he was at liberty, he was to rejoin her in France, at the convent of the Carmelites, at Bethune.

Felton entered Portsmouth about eight o'clock in the morning; the whole population was on foot; drums were beating in the streets and in the port; the troops about to be embarked were marching towards the sea.

He arrived at the palace of the Admiralty, covered with dust, and streaming with perspiration. His countenance, usually so pale, was purple with heat and passion. The sentinel wanted to repulse him, but Felton called to the office of the post, and drawing from his pocket the letter of which he was the bearer—

"A pressing message from the Lord de Winter," said he.

At the name of Lord de Winter, who was known to be one of his grace's most intimate friends, the officer of the post gave orders for Felton to be allowed to pass, who, besides, wore the uniform of a naval officer.

Felton darted into the palace.

At the moment he entered the vestibule, another man was entering likewise, covered with dust, and out of breath, leaving at the gate a post-horse, which, as soon as he had alighted from it, sank down exhausted.

Felton and he addressed Patrick, the duke's confidential valet-de-chambre, at the same moment. Felton named Lord de Winter, the unknown would not name anybody, and asserted that it was to the duke alone he should make himself known. Each was anxious to gain admission before the other.

Patrick, who knew Lord de Winter was in affairs of duty and in relations of friendship with the duke, gave the preference to him who came in his name. The other was forced to wait, and it was easily to be seen how he cursed the delays.

The valet-de-chambre led Felton through a large hall, and introduced him into a closet, where Buckingham, just out of the bath, was finishing his toilet, on which, as at all times, he bestowed extraordinary attention.

"Lieutenant Felton, on the part of the Lord de Winter," said Patrick.

"From Lord de Winter!" repeated Buckingham; "but let him come in."

Felton entered. At that moment, Buckingham was

throwing upon a couch a rich robe-de-chambre worked with gold, to put on a blue velvet doublet embroidered with pearls.

"Why did not the baron come himself?" demanded Buckingham.

"He desired me to tell your grace," replied Felton, "that he very much regretted not having that honour, but that he was prevented by the guard he is obliged to keep at the castle."

"Yes, I know," said Buckingham; "he has a prisoner."

"It is of that prisoner I wish to speak to your grace," replied Felton.

"Well, then, speak!"

"That which I have to say of her can only be heard by yourself, my lord!"

"Leave us, Patrick," said Buckingham, "but remain within the sound of the bell."

Patrick went out.

"We are alone, sir," said Buckingham, "speak."

"My lord," said Felton, "the baron de Winter wrote to you the other day to request you to sign an order of embarkation relative to a young woman. Here it is, my Lord."

"Give it to me," said the Duke.

And, taking it from Felton, he cast a rapid glance over the paper, and perceived that it was the one that had been mentioned to him, he placed it on the table, took a pen, and prepared to sign it.

"I ask your pardon, my lord," said Felton, stopping the Duke: "but does your grace know the true name of this young woman?"

"Yes, I know it."

"And, knowing that real name, my lord," replied Felton, "will you sign it all the same?"

"Doubtless, I will," said Buckingham, "and rather twice than once."

"My lord, Lady de Winter is an angel; you know that she is, and I demand her liberty of you."

"Why, the man must be mad to talk to me in this manner!" said Buckingham.

"My lord, excuse me! I speak as I am able; I restrain myself all I can. But, my lord, think of what you are about to do, and beware of going too far!"

"God pardon me!" cried Buckingham, "I really think the man threatens me!"

"No, my lord, I still pray, and I say to you: one drop of water suffices to make the vase overflow, one slight fault may draw down punishment upon the head spared amidst many crimes."

"Master Felton," said Buckingham, "you will please to withdraw, and place yourself under arrest immediately."

"You shall hear me to the end, my lord. You have seduced this young girl, you have outraged, defiled her; let her go free, and I will require nothing else of you."

"You will require!" said Buckingham, looking at Felton with astonishment, and dwelling upon each syllable of the words as he pronounced them.

"My lord," continued Felton, becoming more excited as he spoke—"my lord, beware! God will punish you hereafter, but I will punish you here!"

"Well! this is too much!" cried Buckingham, making a step towards the door.

Felton barred his passage.

"Withdraw, sir," said Buckingham, "or I will call my attendant, and have you placed in irons."

"Sign, my lord, sign the liberation of Lady de Winter," said Felton, holding a paper to the duke.

"What, by force! you are joking!"

"Sign, my lord!"

"Who waits there?" cried the Duke aloud, and at the same time sprang towards his sword.

But Felton did not give him time to draw it; he held the knife, with which milady had stabbed herself, open in his bosom; at one bound he was upon the duke.

At that moment Patrick entered the room, crying:

"A letter from France, my lord."

"From France!" cried Buckingham, forgetting everything on thinking from whom that letter came.

Felton took advantage of this moment, and plunged the knife into his side up to the handle.

"Ah! traitor!" cried Buckingham, "thou hast killed me!"

"Murder!" screamed Patrick.

Felton cast his eyes round for means of escape, and seeing the door free, he rushed into the next chamber, and precipitated himself towards the staircase; but upon the first step he met Lord de Winter, who, seeing him pale, and stained with blood both on his hands and face, seized him, crying:

"I knew it! I guessed it! but too late by a minute, unfortunate that I am."

Felton made no resistance; Lord de Winter placed him in
the hands of the guards.

At the cry uttered by the Duke, the man whom Felton had
met in the ante-chamber rushed into the closet.

He found the Duke reclining upon a sofa, with his hands
pressed upon the wound.

"Laporte," said the duke in a faint voice, "Laporte, do you
come from her?"

"You will live, milord, you will live!" repeated the faithful
servant of Anne of Austria, on his knees before the duke's
sofa.

"What has she written to me?" said Buckingham, feebly,
streaming with blood, and suppressing his agony to speak of
her he loved; "what has she written to me? Read me her
letter."

"Oh! milord!" said Laporte.

"Obey, Laporte; do you not see I have no time to lose?"

Laporte broke the seal, and placed the letter before the eyes
of the duke; but Buckingham in vain endeavoured to make out
the writing.

"Read!" said he, "read! I can not see, read then! for soon,
perhaps, I shall not hear, and I shall die without knowing
what she has written to me."

Laporte made no more difficulty, and read:

MILORD,—By that which, since I have known you,
I have suffered by you and for you, I conjure you, if you
have any care for my repose, to interrupt those great
armaments which you are preparing against France, to
put an end to a war, of which it is publicly said religion is
the ostensible cause, and of which it is generally whispered, your love for me is the concealed and real cause.
This war may not only bring great catastrophes upon
England and France, but misfortunes upon you, milord,
for which I should never console myself.

Be careful of your life, which is menaced, and which
will be dear to me from the moment I am not obliged
to see an enemy in you.

Your affectionate,

ANNE

Buckingham collected all his remaining strength to listen to the reading of the letter; then, when it was ended, as if he had met with a bitter disappointment,—

"Have you nothing else to say to me, Laporte?" asked he.

"Yes, milord! the Queen charged me to tell you to be very careful, for she has been informed that your assassination would be attempted."

"And is that all?" replied Buckingham, impatiently.

"She likewise charged me to tell you that she still loved you."

"Ah!" said Buckingham, "God be praised! my death, then, will not be to her as the death of a stranger."

Laporte burst into tears.

Buckingham endeavoured to smile a last time; but death arrested his wish, which remained engravened on his brow like a last kiss of love.

At this moment the Duke's surgeon arrived, quite terrified; he was already on board the admiral's ship, from which he had been obliged to be fetched.

He approached the Duke, took his hand, held it for an instant in his own, and letting it fall,—

"All is useless," said he, "he is dead."

As soon as Lord de Winter saw Buckingham was dead, he ran to Felton, whom the soldiers still guarded on the terrace of the palace.

"Miserable wretch!" said he, to the young man, who since the death of Buckingham had regained that coolness and self-possession which never abandoned him; "miserable wretch! what hast thou done?"

"I have avenged myself!" said he.

"Avenged yourself!" said the baron: "rather say that you have served as an instrument to that accursed woman; but I swear to you, that this crime shall be her last crime."

"I don't know what you mean," replied Felton, quietly. I killed the Duke of Buckingham because he twice refused you yourself to appoint me captain; I have punished him for his injustice, that is all."

De Winter, quite stupefied, looked on while the soldiers bound Felton, and could not tell what to think of such insensibility.

One thing alone, however, threw a shade over the pallid brow of Felton. At every noise he heard, the simple Puritan fancied he recognised the step and voice of milady, coming to throw herself into his arms, to accuse herself, and meet death with him.

All at once he started—his eyes became fixed upon a point of the sea. With the eagle glance of a sailor, he had recognised the sail of the sloop, which was directed towards the coast of France.

He grew deadly pale, placed his hand upon his heart, which was breaking, and at once perceived all the treachery.

De Winter followed his look, observed his feelings, and guessed all.

"Be punished alone, in the first place, miserable man!" said Lord de Winter to Felton, who was being dragged away with his eyes turned towards the sea, "but I swear to you, by the memory of my brother whom I loved so much, that your accomplice is not saved."

Felton hung down his head without pronouncing a syllable.

As to Lord de Winter, he descended the stairs rapidly, and went straight to the port.

XVII

The first fear of the King of England, Charles I, on learning the death of the Duke, was that such terrible news might discourage the Rochellais; he endeavoured, says Richelieu in his memoirs, to conceal it from them as long as possible, closing all the ports of his kingdom, and carefully keeping watch that no vessel should go out until the army which Buckingham was getting together, had set sail, taking upon himself, in default of Buckingham, to superintend its departure.

But as he did not think of giving this order till five hours after the event, that is to say, till two o'clock in the afternoon, two vessels had already left the port: the one bearing, as we know, milady, who already anticipated the event, was further confirmed in that belief by seeing the black flag flying at the masthead of the admiral's ship.

As to the second vessel, we will tell hereafter whom it carried, and how it set sail.

During all this time, nothing fresh occurred in the camp at La Rochelle; only the King, who grew weary everywhere but perhaps a little more so in the camp than in any other place, resolved to go incognito and spend the festival of the St. Louis at St. Germain's and asked the Cardinal to order him an escort of twenty musketeers only.

M. de Tréville, upon being informed by his eminence, made up his portmanteau, and as, without knowing the cause, he knew the great desire and even imperative want that his friends had to return to Paris, he fixed upon them, of course, to form part of the escort.

It must be admitted that this impatience to return towards Paris had for cause the danger which Madame Bonacieux would run of meeting at the Convent of Bethune with milady, her mortal enemy. Aramis, therefore, had written immediately to Marie Michon, the seamstress at Tours, who had such fine acquaintances, to obtain from the Queen authority for Madame Bonacieux to leave the convent, and to retire either into Lorraine or Belgium.

At length the escort passed through Paris on the 23rd, in the night; the King thanked M. de Tréville, and permitted him to distribute leaves of absence for four days, upon condition that the favoured parties should not appear in any public place, under penalty of the Bastille.

The first four leaves granted, as may be imagined, were to our four friends. Still further, Athos obtained of M. de Tréville six days instead of four, and introduced into these six days two more nights, for they set out on the 24th, at five o'clock in the evening, and, as a further kindness, M. de Tréville post-dated the leave to the 25th in the morning.

"Good Lord!" said D'Artagnan, who, as we have often said, never doubted of anything—"it appears to me that we are making a great trouble of a very simple thing: in two days I am at Bethune, I present my letter from the Queen to the superior, and I bring back the dear treasure I go to seek, not into Lorraine, not into Belgium, but to Paris; where she will be much better concealed, particularly whilst the Cardinal is at La Rochelle. Remain then where you are, and do not exhaust yourselves with useless fatigue: myself and Planchet that is all that such a simple expedition as this requires."

To this Athos replied quietly:

"We also have money left. But consider, D'Artagnan," added he, in a tone so solemn that it made the young man shudder, "consider that Bethune is a city at which the Cardinal has appointed to meet a woman, who, wherever she goes, brings misery with her. If you had only to deal with four men, D'Artagnan, I would allow you to go alone; you have to do with that woman—we will go, and I hope to God that, with our four lackeys, we may be in sufficient number."

"You terrify me, Athos!" cried D'Artagnan; "my God! what do you fear?"

"Everything!" replied Athos.

On the evening of the 25th, as they were entering Arras, and as D'Artagnan was dismounting at the Golden Gate Inn to drink a glass of wine, a horseman came out of the posting yard, where he had just had a relay, starting off at a gallop, and with a fresh horse, and taking the road to Paris. At the moment he was passing through the gateway into the street, the wind blew open the cloak in which he was enveloped, although it was the month of August, and lifted his hat, which the traveller seized with his hand at the moment it had left his head, and pulled it down eagerly over his eyes.

D'Artagnan, who had his eyes fixed upon this man, became very pale, and let his glass fall.

"What is the matter, monsieur?" said Planchet. "Oh, come, gentlemen, gentlemen! my master is ill!"

The three friends hastened towards D'Artagnan, but, instead of finding him ill, met him running towards his horse. They stopped him at the door.

"Where the devil are you going to now, in this fashion?" cried Athos.

"It is he!" cried D'Artagnan, pale with passion, and with the sweat on his brow, "it is he! let me overtake him!"

"He! but what he?" asked Athos.

"That cursed man, my evil genius, whom I have always met with when threatened by some misfortune—he who accompanied the horrible woman when I met her for the first time—he whom I was seeking when I offended our Athos—he whom I saw on the very morning Madame Bonacieux was carried off! I recognized him when his cloak blew open!"

"The devil!" said Athos musingly.

"To horse, gentlemen! to horse! let us pursue him: we shall overtake him!"

"My dear friend," said Aramis, "remember that it is in an

opposite direction to that in which we are going, that he has a fresh horse, and ours are fatigued, so that we shall disable our own horses without a chance of overtaking him. Let the man go, D'Artagnan; let us save the woman."

"Monsieur, monsieur!" cried a stableman, running out and looking after the unknown—"monsieur, here is a paper which dropped out of your hat! monsieur!"

"Friend," said D'Artagnan, "a half-pistole for that paper!"

"Ma foi! monsieur, with great pleasure! here it is!"

The stableman, delighted with the good day's work he had done, went into the yard again; D'Artagnan unfolded the paper.

"Well?" eagerly demanded all his three friends.

"Nothing but one word!" said D'Artagnan.

"Yes," said Aramis, "but that one word is the name of some town or village."

"Armentières!" read Porthos.

"And that name of a town or village is written in her hand!" cried Athos.

"Come on, then!" said D'Artagnan; "To horse, my friends, to horse!"

And the four friends galloped off on the road to Bethune.

XVIII

Great criminals bear about them a kind of predestination which makes them surmount all obstacles.

It was thus with milady. She passed through the cruisers of both nations, and arrived at Boulogne without accident.

Milady had, likewise, the best of passports—her beauty, her noble appearance, and the liberality with which she distributed her pistoles. Freed from the usual formalities by the affable smile and gallant manners of an old governor of the port, who kissed her hand, she only remained long enough at Boulogne to put into the post a letter, conceived in the following terms:

To His Eminence Monseigneur the Cardinal de Richelieu in his camp before La Rochelle.

Monseigneur, let your eminence be reassured; his grace the Duke of Buckingham will not set out for France.

Boulogne, evening of the 25th.

MILADY DE. . .

P.S.—According to the desire of your eminence, I am going to the Convent of the Carmelites of Bethune, where I will await your orders.

Accordingly, that same evening, milady commenced her journey; night overtook her; she stopped, and slept at an auberge; at five o'clock the next morning she again proceeded, and in three hours after entered Bethune.

She inquired for the Convent of the Carmelites, and went to it immediately.

The superior came out to her; milady showed her the cardinal's order; the abbess assigned her a chamber, and had breakfast served.

After breakfast, the abbess came to pay her a visit. There is very little amusement in the cloister, and the good superior was eager to make acquaintance with her new pensioner.

The abbess looked at her for an instant.

"You are not an enemy of our holy faith?" said she hesitatingly.

"Who—I?" cried milady—"I a Protestant! Oh no! I attest the God who hears us, that, on the contrary, I am a fervent Catholic!"

"Then madame," said the abbess, smiling, "Be reassured; we will do all in our power to make you in love with your captivity. You will find here, moreover, another young woman who is persecuted, no doubt, in consequence of some court intrigue. She is amiable and well-behaved."

"What is her name?"

"She was sent to me by some one of high-rank, under the name of Kitty. I have not endeavoured to discover her other name."

"And when can I see this young lady, for whom I already feel so great a sympathy?" asked milady.

"Why, this evening," said the abbess: "But you have been

travelling these four days, you must stand in need of repose. Go to bed and sleep, at dinner time we will call you."

Milady took leave of the abbess, and went to bed, softly rocked by the ideas of vengeance which the name of Kitty had naturally brought back to her thoughts. She remembered that almost unlimited promise which the Cardinal had given her if she succeeded in her enterprise. She had succeeded, D'Artagnan was in her power.

She was awakened by a soft voice, which sounded at the foot of her bed. She opened her eyes, and saw the abbess accompanied by a young woman, with light hair and a delicate complexion.

The abbess introduced them to each other; then she left the two young women alone.

The novice, seeing milady remained in bed, was about to follow the example of her superior; but milady stopped her.

"How, madame," said she, "I have scarcely seen you, and you already wish to deprive me of your company, upon which I had reckoned a little, I must confess, during the time I have to pass here?"

"No, madame," replied the novice, "only I thought I had chosen my time ill: you were asleep—you are fatigued."

"Well," said milady, "what can people who are asleep wish for? a happy awakening. This awakening you have given me; allow me then to enjoy it at my ease"; and taking her hand, she drew her towards the chair by the bedside.

The novice sat down.

"I think I learned you had suffered persecutions from the Cardinal," continued milady; "that would have been another motive for sympathy between us."

"What, you have likewise been a victim of that wicked priest?"

"Hush!" said milady; "let us not, even here, speak thus of him: almost all my misfortunes arise from my having said nearly what you have said, before a woman whom I thought my friend, and who betrayed me. The Queen herself does not dare to oppose the terrible minister: I have proof that her majesty, notwithstanding her excellent heart, has more than once been obliged to abandon persons who had served her to the anger of his eminence."

"Trust me, madame, the Queen may appear to have abandoned those persons; but we must not put faith in appearances. The more they are persecuted, the more she thinks of them; and often, when they the least expect it, they receive proofs of a kind remembrance."

"Alas!" said milady, "I believe so; the Queen is so good!"

"Oh! you know her, then! that lovely and noble Queen, by your speaking of her thus!" cried the novice warmly.

"That is to say," replied milady, driven into her entrenchments, "that I have not the honour of knowing her personally; but I know a great number of her most intimate friends; I am acquainted with M. de Putange; I met M. Dujart in England; I know M. de Tréville."

"M. de Tréville!" exclaimed the novice, "do you know M. de Tréville? Then you must have met some of his musketeers?"

"All such as he is in the habit of receiving!" replied milady, for whom this conversation began to have a real interest.

"Name a few of those you know, and you will find they are my friends."

"Well!" said milady, a little embarrassed, "I know M. de Sauvigny, M. de Courtviron, M. de Ferrusac."

The novice let her speak, but observing she stopped,—

"Don't you know," said she, "a gentleman of the name of Athos?"

Milady became as pale as the sheets in which she was reclining, and mistress as she was of herself, could not help uttering a cry, seizing the hand of the novice, and devouring her with her looks.

"What is the matter? Good God!" asked the poor woman; "have I said anything that has hurt your feelings?"

"No, no; but the name struck me; because I also have known that gentleman, and it appeared strange to me to meet with a person who appears to know him well. Do you also know D'Artagnan?"

"You know M. D'Artagnan!" cried the novice, in her turn seizing the hands of milady, and fixing her eyes upon her.

"I know you now: you are Madame Bonacieux," said Milady.

The young woman drew back in surprise and terror.

"Oh, do not deny it!"

"Well! yes, madame!" said the novice; "are we rivals?"

The countenance of milady was illuminated by a savage joy.

"Speak, madame!" resumed Madame Bonacieux, with an

energy of which she might not have been thought to be capable, "have you been, or are you, his mistress?"

"Oh, no!" cried milady, with a tone that admitted no doubt of her truth; "never! never!"

"I believe you," said Madame Bonacieux; "but why, then, did you cry out so?"

"Can you not understand that M. d'Artagnan, being my friend, might take me into his confidence?"

"Indeed!"

"Do you not perceive that I know all? Your being carried off from the little house at St. Germain, his despair, that of his friends, and their useless inquiries up to this moment!"

"Then you know what I have suffered," said Madame Bonacieux.

"And that," continued Madame Bonacieux, "my punishment is drawing to a close: tomorrow, this evening, perhaps, I shall see him again; and then the past will no longer exist."

"This evening?" asked milady, roused from her reverie by these words; "Oh, I cannot believe you!"

"Well, read then!" said the unhappy young woman, in the excess of her pride and joy, presenting a letter to milady.

"Humph! The writing of Madame de Chevreuse!" said milady to herself. "Ah! I always thought there was some intelligence carried on on that side!" And she greedily read the following few lines:

> MY DEAR CHILD,—Hold yourself in readiness. Our friend will see you soon, and he will only see you to release you from that imprisonment in which your safety required you should be concealed. Prepare, then, for your departure, and never despair of us.
>
> Our charming Gascon has just proved himself as brave and faithful as ever. Tell him that certain parties are grateful to him for the warning he has given.

"Yes, yes," said milady, "the letter is precise. Do you know what that warning was?"

"No; I only suspect he has warned the Queen, against some fresh machinations of the Cardinal."

"Yes, that's it, no doubt!" said milady, returning the letter to Madame Bonacieux, and allowing her head to sink in a pensive manner upon her bosom.

At that moment the galloping of a horse was heard.

"Oh!" cried Madame Bonacieux, darting to the window: "can it be he!"

In fact, the door opened, and the superior entered.

"A gentleman to speak with you, milady," she said.

"I will leave you with this stranger; but as soon as he is gone, if you will permit me, I will return," said Madame Bonacieux.

"Certainly! I beg you will."

The superior and Madame Bonacieux retired.

Milady was left alone, with her eyes fixed upon the door. An instant after, the jingling of spurs was heard upon the stairs, steps drew near, the door opened, and a man appeared.

Milady uttered a cry of joy; this man was the Count of Rochefort. His whispered message took but a few seconds and then he was gone.

Rochefort had scarcely departed, when Madame Bonacieux re-entered. She found milady with a smiling countenance.

"Well," said the young woman, "what you dreaded has happened; this evening, or tomorrow, the Cardinal will send someone to take you away!"

"Who told you that, my dear?" asked milady.

"I heard it from the mouth of the messenger himself."

Milady arose, went to the door, opened it, looked in the corridor, and then returned and seated herself close to Madame Bonacieux.

"Then," said she, "he has well played his part."

"Who has?"

"He who just now presented himself to the abbess as a messenger from the Cardinal."

"It was, then, a part he was playing?"

"Yes, my dear."

"That man, then was not—"

"That man," said milady, lowering her voice, 'is my brother!"

"Your brother!" said Madame Bonacieux.

"Mind no one must know this secret, my dear, but yourself. If you reveal it to any one, whatever, I shall be lost, and perhaps you likewise!"

"Oh! good God!"

"Listen to me; this is what has happened. My brother, who was coming to my assistance, to take me away by force, if it were necessary, met with the emissary of the Cardinal, who was coming in search of me. He followed him. When they arrived at a solitary and retired part of the road, he drew his sword and required the messenger to deliver up to him the papers of which he was the bearer; the messenger resisted; my brother killed him.

"Oh!" said Madame Bonacieux, with a shudder.

"Remember, that was the only means. Then my brother determined to substitute cunning by force. He took the papers, and presented himself here as the emissary of the Cardinal, and in an hour or two a carriage will come to take me away by the orders of his eminence."

"I understand: your brother sends this carriage."

"Exactly so; but that is not all. That letter you have received and which you believe to be from Madame de Chevreuse—"

"Well?"

"It is a forgery."

"How can that be?"

"Yes, a forgery; it is a snare to prevent your making any resistance when the persons come to fetch you."

"But it is D'Artagnan that will come!"

"Do not deceive yourself. D'Artagnan and his friends are detained at the siege of La Rochelle."

"How do you know that?"

"My brother met some emissaries of the Cardinal in the uniform of musketeers. You would have been summoned, to the gate, you would have thought you went to meet friends you would have been carried off, and conducted back again to Paris."

"Oh! good God! My senses fail me amidst such a chaos of iniquities. I feel, if this continues," said Madame Bonacieux, raising her hands to her forehead, "I shall go mad."

"Stop—"

"What?"

"I hear a horse's step; it is my brother setting off again. I should like to offer him a last salute. Come?"

Milady opened the window, and made a sign to Madame Bonacieux to join her. The young woman complied.

Rochefort passed at a gallop.

"Adieu, brother!" cried milady.

The chevalier raised his head, saw the two young women,

and without stopping, waved his hand in a friendly way to milady.

"Dear, good George!" said she, closing the window with an expression of countenance full of affection and melancholy.

And she resumed her seat, as if plunged in reflections entirely personal.

"Dear lady," said Madame Bonacieux, "pardon me for interrupting you; but what do you advise me to do?"

"In the first place," said milady, "it is possible that I may be deceived, and D'Artagnan and his friends may really come to your assistance."

"Oh! that would be too much!" cried Madame Bonacieux; "so much happiness is not destined for me!"

"Then you perceive it would be only a question of time, a sort of race, which should arrive first. If your friends are the more speedy, you will be saved; if the satellites of the Cardinal are so, you will be lost!"

"Oh! yes, yes! lost beyond redemption! What am I to do? what am I to do?"

"There would be a very simple means, very natural—"

"What? Speak!"

"To wait, concealed in the neighbourhood, until you have satisfied yourself who the men were who came to ask for you."

"But where can I wait?"

"Oh! there is no difficulty in that; I shall stop and conceal myself at a few leagues from hence, until my brother can rejoin me. Well! I can take you with me; we can conceal ourselves, and wait together."

"But I shall not be allowed to go; I am almost a prisoner here."

"As I am supposed to go in consequence of an order from the Cardinal, no one will believe you are anxious to follow me."

"Well?"

"Well! the carriage is at the door, you bid me adieu, you get upon the step to embrace me, a last time; my brother's servant, who comes to fetch me, is told how to proceed; he makes a sign to the postillion, and we set off at a gallop."

"But D'Artagnan! D'Artagnan! If he should come!"

"Well! shall we not know it?"

"How?"

"Nothing more easy. We will send my brother's servant

back to Bethune, and, as I told you we can trust in him, he shall assume a disguise, and place himself in front of the convent. If the emissaries of the Cardinal arrive, he will take no notice; if they are M. D'Artagnan and his friend, he will bring them to us."

"He knows them, then?"

"Doubtless he does. Has he not seen M. D'Artagnan at my house?"

"Oh, yes, yes, you are right; in this way all may go well—all may be for the best, but do not go far from this place—"

"Seven or eight leagues at most; we will keep on the frontiers, for instance; and at the first alarm, we can leave France."

"But if they come?"

"My brother's carriage will be here first."

"If I should happen to be at any distance from you when the carriage comes for you; at dinner or supper, for instance?"

"Do one thing."

"What is that?"

"Tell your good superior, that in order that we may be as much together as possible, you beg her to allow you to take your meals with me."

"Oh, delightful! in this way, we shall not be separated for an instant."

"Well! go down to her, then, to make your request. I feel my head a little confused: I will take a turn in the garden."

And the two women parted, exchanging affectionate smiles.

Milady had told the truth—her head was confused; for her ill-arranged plans clashed against each other like a chaos. She saw vaguely into futurity; but she stood in need of a little silence and quiet to give all her ideas, at present in confusion, distinct form and a regular plan.

What was most pressing was to get Madame Bonacieux away, and convey her to a place of safety, and there, matters so falling out, make her a hostage. The principal thing for her then was to keep Madame Bonacieux in her power. Madame Bonacieux was the very life of D'Artagnan; more than his life was the life of the woman he loved.

Whilst revolving all this in her mind, she cast her eyes around her, and arranged the topography of the garden in her head.

At the end of an hour, she heard a soft voice calling her; it was Madame de Bonacieux's. The good abbess had naturally consented to her request; and as a commencement, they were to sup together.

On reaching the courtyard, they heard the noise of a carriage, which stopped at the gate.

Milady listened.

"It is the one my brother sends for us."

"Oh! my God!"

"Come; come! courage!"

The bell of the convent gate was rung—milady was not mistaken.

"Go up to your chamber," said she to Madame Bonacieux; "you have perhaps some jewels you would like to take with you."

"I have his letters," said she.

"Well! go and fetch them, and come to my apartment; we will snatch some supper; we shall perhaps travel part of the night, and must keep our strength up."

"Great God!" said Madame Bonacieux, placing her hand upon her bosom; "my heart beats so I cannot walk."

"Courage, my dear, courage, remember that in a quarter of an hour you will be safe; and think that what you are about to do is for his sake."

"Yes, yes, everything for his sake. You have restored my courage by a single word; go up, I will be with you directly."

Milady ran up to her apartment quickly; she there found Rochefort's lackey, and gave him instructions.

He was to wait at the gate; if by chance, the musketeers should appear, the carriage was to set off as fast as possible, pass round the convent, and go and wait for milady at a little village which was situated at the other side of the wood. In this case milady was to cross the garden and gain the village on foot.

If the musketeers did not appear, things were to go on as had been agreed; Madame Bonacieux was to get into the carriage as if to bid her adieu, and she was to take away Madame Bonacieux.

Madame Bonacieux came in; and, to remove all suspicion, if she had any, milady repeated to the lackey, before her, the latter part of her instructions.

Milady made some questions about the carriage; it was a

chaise with three horses, driven by a postillion; Rochefort's
lackey preceded it, as a courier.

Milady was wrong in fearing that Madame Bonacieux
would have any suspicions; the poor young woman was too
pure to suppose that any female could be guilty of such per-
fidy; besides, the name of the Countess de Winter, which
she had heard the abbess pronounce, was perfectly unknown
to her, and she was even ignorant that a woman had had so
great and so fatal a share in the misfortune of her life.

"You see," said she, when the lackey was gone out, "everything is ready. The abbess suspects nothing, and believes, that
I am fetched by the orders of the cardinal. The man is gone
to give his last orders; take a mouthful to eat, drink half a
glass of wine, and let us be gone;" Madame Bonacieux ate a
few mouthfuls mechanically, and just touched the glass with
her lips.

"Come! Come!" said milady, lifting hers to her mouth, "do
as I do."

But at the moment the glass touched her lips, her hand remained suspended; she heard something in the road which
sounded like the rattling of a distant gallop, and which drew
nearer; and, almost at the same time, she heard the neighing
of horses.

This noise acted upon her joy like the storm which awak-
ens the sleeper in the midst of a happy dream; she grew pale,
and ran to the window, whilst Madame Bonacieux, rising all
in a tremble, supported herself upon her chair to avoid falling.

Nothing was yet to be seen, only they heard the galloping
draw nearer.

"Oh! my God!" said Madame Bonacieux, "what is that
noise?"

"That of either our friends or our enemies," said milady,
with her terrible coolness; "stay where you are, I will tell
you."

The noise became so distinct that the horses might be
counted by the sound of their hooves.

Milady looked as if her eyes would start; it was just light
enough to allow her to see those who were coming.

All at once, at the turning of the road, she saw the glitter
of laced hats and the waving of feathers; she counted two,
then five, then eight horsemen; one of them preceded the rest
by double the length of his horse.

Milady uttered a stifled groan. In the first horseman she recognised D'Artagnan.

"Oh! heavens! oh! heavens!" cried Madame Bonacieux, "what is it? what is it?"

"It is the uniform of the Cardinal's guards, not an instant to be lost! Let us fly! let us fly!"

"Oh! yes! let us fly!" repeated Madame Bonacieux, but without being able to make a step, fixed to the spot she stood on by terror.

They heard the horsemen pass under the windows.

"Come, then! why, come, then!" cried milady, endeavouring to drag her along by the arm. "Thanks to the garden, we yet can fly; I have the key; but, make haste! In five minutes it will be too late!"

Madame Bonacieux endeavoured to walk, made two steps and sank upon her knees.

Milady endeavoured to raise and carry her, but could not succeed.

At this moment they heard the rolling of the carriage which at the approach of the musketeers, set off at a gallop. Then three or four shots were fired.

"For the last time, will you come?" cried milady.

"Oh! heaven! oh! heaven! you see my strength fails me, you see plainly I cannot walk; fly alone!"

"Fly alone! and leave you here! no, no, never!" cried milady.

All at once she remained still, a livid flash darted from her eyes; she ran to the table, poured into Madame Bonacieux's glass the contents of a ring, which she opened with singular quickness.

It was a grain of a reddish colour, which melted immediately. Then, taking the glass with a firm hand—

"Drink," said she, "this wine will give you strength, drink!"

And she put the glass to the lips of the young woman, who drank mechanically.

"This is not the way that I wished to avenge myself," said milady, replacing the glass upon the table with an infernal smile, "but ma foi! we do what we can!"

And she rushed out of the room.

Madame Bonacieux saw her go without being able to follow her; she was like those people who dream they are pursued, and who in vain endeavour to walk.

A few moments passed, a great noise was heard at the gate; every instant Madame Bonacieux expected to see milady; but she did not return.

Several times, with terror, no doubt, the cold sweat burst from her burning brow.

At length she heard the grating of the hinges of the opening gates, the noise of boots and spurs resounded on the stair; there was a great murmur of voices, which continued to draw near, and amongst which it appeared to her she heard her own name pronounced.

All at once she uttered a loud cry of joy, and darted towards the door, she had recognized the voice of D'Artagnan.

"D'Artagnan! D'Artagnan!" cried she, "is it you? This way! this way!"

"Constance! Constance!" replied the young man, "where are you? where are you?"

At the same moment, the door of the cell yielded to a shock, rather than was opened; several men rushed into the chamber; Madame Bonacieux had sunk into a fauteuil without the power of moving.

D'Artagnan threw a yet smoking pistol from his hand, and fell on his knees before his mistress; Athos replaced his in his belt; Porthos and Aramis, who held their drawn swords in their hands, returned them to their scabbards.

"Oh! D'Artagnan! my beloved D'Artagnan! thou art come then, at last, thou hast not deceived me! it is indeed thee!"

"Yes, yes, dear Constance! united at last!"

"Oh! it was in vain she told me you would not come. I hoped silently; I was not willing to fly; oh! how rightly I have done! how happy I am!"

At this word, she, Athos, who had seated himself quietly started up.

"She! what she?" asked D'Artagnan.

"Why, my companion; she who, from friendship for me wished to take me from my persecutors; she who, mistaking you for the Cardinal's guards, has just fled away."

"Your companion!" cried D'Artagnan becoming more pale than the white veil of his mistress, "of what companion are you speaking, dear Constance?"

"Of her whose carriage was at the gate, of a woman who calls herself your friend, of a woman to whom you have told everything."

"But her name, her name!" cried D'Artagnan; "my God! can you not remember her name?"

"Yes, it was pronounced before me once; stop—but—it is very strange—oh! my God! my head swims—I cannot see!"

"Help! help! my friends! her hands are icy cold," cried D'Artagnan, "she will faint! great God, she is losing her senses!"

Whilst Porthos was calling for help with all the power of his strong voice, Aramis ran to the table to get a glass of water; but he stopped at seeing the horrible alteration that had taken place in the countenance of Athos, who standing before the table, his hair rising from his head, his eyes fixed in stupor, was looking at one of the glasses and appeared a prey to the most horrible doubt.

"Oh!" said Athos, "oh! no, it is impossible. God would not permit such a crime!"

"Water! water!" cried D'Artagnan, "water!"

"Oh! poor woman! poor woman!" murmured Athos in a broken voice.

Madame Bonacieux opened her eyes under the kisses of D'Artagnan.

"She revives!" cried the young man. "Oh! my God! my God! I thank Thee!"

"Madame!" said Athos, "madame, in the name of heaven, whose empty glass is this?"

"Mine, monsieur," said the young woman in a dying voice.

"But who poured out the wine for you that was in this glass?"

"She."

"But who was that she?"

"Oh! I remember," said Madame Bonacieux, "the Countess de Winter."

The four friends uttered one and the same cry, but that of Athos dominated over all the rest.

At that moment the countenance of Madame Bonacieux became livid, a fearful agony pervaded her frame, and she sank panting into the arms of Porthos and Aramis.

"D'Artagnan! D'Artagnan! where are thou? Do not quit me, thou seest that I am dying!" cried Madame Bonacieux.

D'Artagnan hastened to her.

Her beautiful face was distorted with agony, her glassy eyes were fixed, a convulsive shuddering shook her whole body, the sweat flowed from her brow.

"In the name of heaven, run, call: Aramis! Porthos! call for help."

"Useless!" said Athos, "useless! for the poison which she pours out there is no counter-poison!"

"Yes! help!" murmured Madame Bonacieux, "help!"

Then, collecting all her strength, she took the head of the young man between her hands, looked at him for an instant as if her whole soul passed in that look, and, with a sobbing cry, pressed her lips to his.

"Constance! Constance!" cried D'Artagnan wildly.

A sigh escaped from the mouth of Madame Bonacieux, and dwelt for an instant on the lips of D'Artagnan—that sigh was the soul so chaste and so loving reascending to heaven.

D'Artagnan held nothing but a corpse pressed in his arms.

The young man uttered a cry and fell by the side of his mistress as pale and as senseless as she was.

Porthos wept, Aramis pointed towards heaven, Athos made the sign of the cross.

At that moment a man appeared in the doorway almost as pale as those in the chamber, looked round him and saw Madame Bonacieux dead, and D'Artagnan fainting.

"I was not deceived," said he; "Here is M. D'Artagnan and you are his friends, Messieurs Athos, Porthos, and Aramis."

The persons whose names were thus pronounced looked at the stranger with astonishment, all three thought they knew him.

"Gentlemen," resumed the newcomer, "you are, as I am, in search of a woman, who," added he, with a terrible smile, "must have passed this way, for I see a corpse!"

The three friends remained mute, for although the voice as well as the countenance reminded them of someone they had seen, they could not remember under what circumstances.

"Gentlemen," continued the stranger, "since you do not recognise a man who probably owes his life to you twice, I must name myself: I am the Lord de Winter, brother-in-law of that woman."

The three friends uttered a cry of surprise.

Athos rose, and offering his hand,—

"You are welcome, milord," said he, "you are one of us."

"You see!" said Athos, pointing to Madame Bonacieux dead, and to D'Artagnan, whom Porthos and Aramis were endeavouring to recall to life.

"Are they both dead?" asked Lord de Winter, sternly.

At that moment D'Artagnan opened his eyes.

He tore himself from the arms of Porthos and Aramis and threw himself like a madman on the corpse of his mistress.

Athos rose, walked towards his friend with a slow and solemn step, embraced him tenderly, and as he burst into violent sobs, he said to him, with his noble and persuasive voice:

"Friend, be a man:—women weep for the dead, men avenge them!" And he drew away his friend, affectionate as a father, consoling as a priest, great as a man who has suffered much.

All five, followed by their lackeys, leading their horses, took their way to the town of Bethune, and stopped before the first auberge they came to.

"But," said D'Artagnan, "shall we not pursue that woman?"

"Presently," said Athos; "I have measures to take."

"She will escape us," replied the young man; "she will escape us; and it will be your fault, Athos."

"I will be accountable for her," said Athos.

Lord de Winter believed he spoke in this manner to soothe the grief of D'Artagnan.

"Now, gentlemen," said Athos, when he had ascertained there were five chambers disengaged in the hotel, "let every one retire to his own apartment; I take charge of everything, be all of you at ease."

"It appears, however," said Lord de Winter, "that if there be any measures to take against the countess, it particularly concerns me: she is my sister-in-law."

"And I,"—said Athos,—"she is my wife!"

D'Artagnan smiled, for he was satisfied Athos was sure of his vengeance, when he revealed such a secret as that; Porthos and Aramis looked at each other, and changed colour. Lord de Winter thought Athos was mad.

"Now, all retire to your chambers," said Athos; "and leave me to act. You must perceive that in my quality of a husband this concerns me in particular. Only D'Artagnan, if you have not lost it, give me the piece of paper which fell from that man's hat, upon which is written the name of the village of—"

"Ah!" said D'Artagnan, "I comprehend now; that name written in her hand."

"You see, then," said Athos, "there is a God in heaven, still!"

XIX

At eight o'clock in the evening, Athos ordered the horses to be saddled.

In an instant all five were ready. Athos came down the last, and found D'Artagnan already mounted.

"Patience!" cried Athos; "one of our party is still wanting."

The four horsemen looked round them with astonishment, for they sought uselessly in their minds who this other person they wanted could be.

At this moment Planchet brought out Athos' horse; the musketeer leaped lightly into the saddle.

"Wait for me," cried he; "I will soon be back"; and set off at a gallop.

In a quarter of an hour he returned, accompanied by a tall man, masked, and enveloped in a large red cloak.

Lord de Winter and the three musketeers looked at each other inquiringly. None of them could give the others any information, for all were ignorant who this man could be; nevertheless, they felt convinced that this ought to be so, as it was done by Athos.

At nine o'clock, guided by Planchet, the little cavalcade set out, taking the route the carriage had taken.

It was a stormy and dark night; vast clouds covered the heavens concealing the stars; the moon would not rise much before midnight.

Several times Lord de Winter, Porthos, or Aramis, endeavoured to enter into conversation with the man in the red cloak; but to every interrogation put to him he bowed, without making any reply.

A lightning flash enlightened all around them; Grimaud extended his arm, and by the blue splendour of the serpent of fire they distinguished a little isolated house, on the banks of the river, within a hundred paces of a ferry.

A light was seen at one window.

Athos sprang from his horse, gave the bridle to Grimaud, and advanced towards the window, after having made a sign to the rest of the troop to go towards the door.

The little house was surrounded by a low quickset hedge of two or three feet high; Athos sprang over the hedge, and went up to the window, which was without shutters, but had the half-curtain drawn closely.

By the light of a lamp he saw a woman enveloped in a mantle of a dark colour, seated upon a joint-stool near the dying embers of a fire; her elbows were placed upon a mean table, and she leant her head upon her two hands, which were white as ivory.

At this moment one of the horses neighed; milady raised her head, saw the pale face of Athos close to the window, and screamed with terror.

Athos, perceiving that she knew him, pushed the window with his knee and hand; it yielded—the frame and glass were broken to slivers.

And Athos, like the spectre of vengeance, sprang into the room.

Milady rushed to the door and opened it; but, still more pale and menacing than Athos, D'Artagnan stood on the sill of it.

Milady drew back, uttering a cry; D'Artagnan, believing she might have means of flight, and fearing she could escape, drew a pistol from his belt; but Athos raised his hand.

"Put back that weapon, D'Artagnan," said he; "this woman must be judged, not assassinated. Wait but a little my friend, and you shall be satisfied. Come in, gentlemen."

D'Artagnan obeyed, for Athos had the solemn voice and the powerful gesture of a judge sent by the Lord Himself. Behind D'Artagnan, entered Porthos, Aramis, Lord de Winter and the man in the red cloak.

The four lackeys guarded the door and the window.

Milady had sunk into a chair, with her hands extended, as if to conjure away this terrible apparition. On perceiving her brother-in-law, an agonized cry of surprise and fright burst from her lips.

"What do you want?" screamed milady.

"We want," said Athos, "Charlotte Backson, who first was called Countess de la Fère, and afterwards Lady de Winter, Baroness de Sheffield."

"That is I! that is I!" murmured milady, in extreme terror; "what do you want with me?"

"We want to judge you according to your crime," said Athos: "You shall be free to defend yourself; justify yourself if you can. Monsieur D'Artagnan, it is for you to accuse her first."

D'Artagnan advanced.

"Before God and before men," said he, "I accuse this woman of having poisoned Constance Bonacieux, who died yesterday evening."

He turned towards Porthos and Aramis.

"We bear witness to this," said the two musketeers, with one voice.

"It is your turn, milord," said Athos.

The baron came forward.

"Before God and before men," said he, "I accuse this woman of having been the means of the assassination of the Duke of Buckingham."

A shudder crept through the frames of the judges at the revelation of such unheard-of crimes.

"That is not all," resumed Lord de Winter; "my brother, who made you his heir, died in three hours, of a strange disorder, which left livid traces behind it all over the body. Sister, how did your husband die?"

"Horror! horror!" cried Porthos and Aramis.

"Assassin of Buckingham, assassin of my brother, I demand justice upon you, and I swear that if it be not granted to me, I will execute it myself."

And Lord de Winter ranged himself by the side of D'Artagnan, leaving the place free for another accuser.

"It is my turn," said Athos, himself trembling as a lion trembles at the sight of the serpent; "it is my turn. I married that woman when she was a young girl: I married her in opposition to the wishes of all my family; I gave her my wealth, I gave her my name; and one day I discovered that this woman was branded; this woman was marked with a fleur-de-lis on her left shoulder."

"Oh!" said milady, "I defy you to find any tribunal which pronounced such an infamous sentence against me. I defy you to find him who executed it."

"Silence!" cried a hollow voice. "It is for me to reply to that!"

"What man is that? what man is that?" cried milady.

All eyes turned towards this man; for to all except Athos he was unknown.

After having approached milady with a slow and solemn step, so that the table alone separated them, the unknown took off his mask.

Milady for some time examined with increasing terror that pale face, enframed in its black hair, beard and whiskers, the only expression of which was icy impassibility—all at once—

"Oh! no! no!" cried she, rising and retreating to the very wall;—"no, no! it is an infernal apparition! It cannot be he! Help, help!" screamed she, turning towards the wall, as if she would tear an opening with her hands.

"Who are you, then?" cried all the witnesses of this scene.

"Ask that woman," said the man in the red cloak; "for you may plainly see she knows me"

"The executioner of Lille!" cried milady, a prey to wild terror, and clinging with her hands to the wall to avoid falling.

Everyone drew back, so that the man in the red cloak remained standing alone in the middle of the room.

"This woman was once a nun in the convent of the Benedictines of Templemar, where a young priest was chaplain. She undertook his seduction. To fly together, money was necessary, but neither had any. The priest stole the sacred vessels, and sold them; but as they were preparing to escape, both were arrested. Eight days later she escaped. But as the executioner of Lille, I was obliged to brand the guilty one; and he was my brother!

"I then swore that this woman should share his punishment. I tracked her down, and imprinted on her the same disgraceful mark that I had imprinted on. my poor brother. But he in turn succeeded in escaping; I was accused of complicity, and sentenced to remain in his place till he should be again a prisoner. My poor brother, ignorant of this, rejoined this woman, and they fled into Berry, where he obtained a curacy. She passed for his sister.

"The lord of the estate became enamoured of her. She quitted him she had ruined for him she was destined to ruin, and became the Comtesse de la Fère—"

All eyes turned to Athos, whose real name this was, and who made a sign that all was true.

"Then," resumed the executioner, "mad, desperate, determined to get rid of an existence from which she had stolen everything, both honor and happiness, my poor brother returned to Lille. Learning the sentence which had condemned me in his place, he surrendered, and hanged himself that same night from the iron bar of the loophole of his prison. As soon as the identity of my brother was proved, I was set at liberty.

"That is the cause for which she was branded."

Athos stretched out his hand towards her.

"Charlotte Backson, Countess de la Fère, Milady de Winter," said he, "your crimes have wearied men on earth and God in heaven. If you know any prayer, say it! for you are condemned and you shall die."

Lord de Winter, D'Artagnan, Athos, Porthos, and Aramis, went out close behind her and the executioner. The lackeys followed their masters, and the chamber was left solitary, with its broken window, its open door, and its smoky lamp burning dimly on the table.

It was midnight; the moon, lessened by its decline and reddened by the last traces of the storm, arose behind the little town of Armentières. From time to time a broad sheet of lightning opened the horizon in its whole width, darting like a serpent over the black mass of trees.

Two of the lackeys now led, or rather dragged, milady by her arms; the executioner walked behind her, and Lord de Winter, D'Artagnan, Porthos, and Aramis walked behind the executioner. Planchet and Bazin came last.

The two lackeys led milady to the banks of the river. Her mouth was mute, but her eyes spoke with their inexpressible eloquence, supplicating by turns each of those she looked at.

Being a few paces in advance, she whispered to the lackeys; "A thousand pistoles to each of you; if you will assist my escape; but if you deliver me up to your masters, I have near at hand, avengers who will make you pay for my death, very dearly."

Grimaud hesitated; Mousqueton trembled in all his members.

Athos, who heard milady's voice, came sharply up; Lord de Winter did the same.

"Change these lackeys," said he, "she has spoken to them, they are no longer safe."

Planchet and Bazin were called forward, and took the place of Grimaud and Mousqueton.

When they arrived on the banks of the river, the executioner approached milady, and bound her hands and feet.

"Oh! my God!" cried she, "my God! are you going to drown me?"

These cries had something so heart-rending in them, that M. D'Artagnan, who had been at first the most eager in pursuit of milady, sank down on the stump of a tree, and leant down his head, covering his ears with the palms of his hands; and yet, notwithstanding, he could not help hearing her cry and threaten.

D'Artagnan was the youngest of all these men; his heart failed him.

"Oh! I cannot behold this frightful spectacle!" said he; "I cannot consent that this woman should die thus."

Milady heard these few words, and caught at a shadow of hope.

"D'Artagnan! D'Artagnan!" cried she, "remember that I loved you!"

The young man rose, and made a step towards her.

But Athos arose, likewise, drew his sword, and placed himself between them.

"One step further, M. D'Artagnan," said he, "and, dearly as I love you, we cross swords."

M. D'Artagnan sank on his knees and prayed.

Athos made a step forward towards milady.

"I pardon you," said he, "the ill you have done me; I pardon you for my blasted future, my lost honour, my defiled love. Die in peace!"

Lord de Winter advanced in his turn.

"I pardon you," said he, "the poisoning of my brother, the assassination of his grace the Duke of Buckingham; I pardon you the death of poor Felton! I pardon you the attempts upon my own person. Die in peace."

"And I," said D'Artagnan. "Pardon me, madame, for having by a trick, unworthy of a gentleman, provoked your anger; and I, in exchange, pardon you the murder of my poor love, and your cruel vengeance against me. I pardon you, and I weep for you. Die in peace."

"I am lost!" murmured milady in English. "I must die!"

The boat moved off towards the left-hand shore of the Lys, bearing the guilty woman and the executioner; all the others remained on the right-hand bank, where they fell on their knees.

The boat glided along the ferry-rope under the shadow of a pale cloud which hung over the water at the moment.

The troop of friends saw it gain the opposite bank! the persons cut the red-tinted horizon with a black shade.

Milady, during the passage, had contrived to untie the cord which fastened her feet: on coming near to the bank, she jumped lightly on shore and took flight.

But the soil was moist: on gaining the top of the bank, she slipped and fell upon her knees.

Then they saw from the other bank the executioner raise both his arms slowly, a moonbeam fell upon the blade of the large sword, the two arms fell with a sudden force.

The executioner then took off his red cloak, spread it upon the ground, laid the body in it, tied all up with the four corners, lifted it on to his back, and got into the boat again.

When arrived in the middle of the stream, he stopped the boat, and suspending his burden over the water,—

"Let the justice of God be done!" cried he with a loud voice. And he let the body drop into the depths of the waters, which closed over it.

XX

The return to La Rochelle was profoundly dull. Our four friends, in particular, astonished their comrades; they travelled together, side by side, with spiritless eyes and heads depressed. Athos alone, from time to time, raised his expansive brow; a flash kindled in his eyes, and a bitter smile passed over his lips; then, like his comrades, he sank again into his reveries.

As soon as the escort arrived in any city, when they had conducted the King to his quarters, the four friends either retired to their own or to some secluded cabaret, where they neither drank nor played; they only conversed in a low voice, looking around attentively that no one overheard them. One day, when the King had halted to fly the magpie, and the four friends, according to their custom, instead of following the sport, had stopped at a cabaret on the high road, a man, coming from La Rochelle on horseback, pulled up at the door to drink a glass of wine, and darted a searching glance into the chamber in which the four musketeers were sitting.

"Hulloa! Monsieur D'Artagnan!" said he, "is not that you I see yonder?"

D'Artagnan raised his head and uttered a cry of joy. It was the man he called his phantom, it was his unknown of Meung, of the Rue des Fossoyeurs and of Arras.

D'Artagnan drew his sword, and sprang towards the door.

But this time, instead of avoiding him, the unknown jumped from his horse, and advanced to meet D'Artagnan.

"Ah! monsieur!" said the young man, "I have met with you, then, at last! this time, I will answer for it, you shall not escape me!"

"Neither is it my intention, monsieur, for this time I was seeking you; in the name of the King, I arrest you."

"How! what do you say?" cried D'Artagnan.

"I say that you must surrender your sword to me, monsieur, and that without resistance; the safety of your head depends upon your compliance."

"Who are you, then?" demanded D'Artagnan, lowering the point of his sword, but without yet surrendering it.

"I am the Chevalier de Rochefort," answered the other, "the equerry of monsieur the Cardinal de Richelieu, and I have orders to conduct you to his eminence."

"We are returning to his eminence, Monsieur le Chevalier," said Athos, advancing; "and you will please to accept the word of M. D'Artagnan, that he will go straight to La Rochelle."

"I must place him in the hands of guards who will take him to the camp."

"We will be his guards, monsieur, upon our words, as gentlemen; but, upon our words as gentlemen, likewise," added Athos, knitting his brow, "M. D'Artagnan shall not leave us."

On returning in the evening to his quarters at the bridge of La Pierre, the cardinal found D'Artagnan, without his sword, and the three musketeers armed, standing before the door of the house.

His eminence went to the chamber which served him as a closet, and made a sign to Rochefort to bring in the young musketeer.

Rochefort obeyed and retired.

Richelieu remained standing, leaning against the mantelpiece; a table was between him and D'Artagnan.

"Monsieur," said the Cardinal, "you have been arrested by my orders."

"So I have been informed, monseigneur."

"Do you know why?"

"If monseigneur will have the goodness to tell me, in the first place, what crimes are imputed to me, I will then tell your eminence what I have really done."

"Crimes are imputed to you that have brought down much more lofty heads than yours, monsieur," said the Cardinal.

"What are they, monseigneur?" said D'Artagnan, with a calmness that astonished the Cardinal himself.

"You are charged with having corresponded with the enemies of the kingdom; you are charged with having surprised state secrets; you are charged with having endeavoured to thwart the plans of your general."

"And who charged me with this, monseigneur?" said D'Artagnan, who had no doubt the accusation came from milady—"a woman branded by the justice of the country—a woman who has espoused one man in France and another in England—a woman who poisoned her second husband, and who attempted both to poison and assassinate me!"

"What is all this, monsieur?" cried the Cardinal astonished, "and what woman are you speaking of thus?"

"Of Milady de Winter," replied D'Artagnan—"yes, of Milady de Winter, of whose crimes your eminence is doubtless ignorant because you have honoured her with your confidence."

"Monsieur," said the Cardinal, "if Milady de Winter has committed the crimes you lay to her charge, she shall be punished."

"She is punished, monseigneur."

"And who has punished her?"

"We have."

"Is she in prison?"

"She is dead."

"Dead!" repeated the Cardinal, who could not believe what he heard—"dead! Did you say she was dead?"

D'Artagnan then related the poisoning of Madame Bonacieux in the convent of the Carmelites of Bethune, the trial in the solitary house, and the execution on the banks of the Lys.

A shudder crept through the body of the Cardinal, who, it may be observed, was not easily made to shudder.

But all at once, as if undergoing the influence of a secret thought, the countenance of the Cardinal, till that moment gloomy, cleared up by degrees, and received perfect serenity.

"So," said the Cardinal, in a tone that contrasted strongly with the severity of his words, "you have constituted yourselves judges, without remembering that they who punish without licence to punish are assassins?"

"Another might reply that he had his pardon in his pocket. I will content myself with saying: issue your orders, monseigneur; I am ready."

"Your pardon?" said Richelieu, surprised.

"Yes, monseigneur," said D'Artagnan.

"And signed by whom—by the King?"

And the Cardinal pronounced these words with a singular expression of contempt.

"No; by your eminence."

"By me? You must be mad, monsieur!"

"Monseigneur will doubtless recognize his own writing."

And D'Artagnan presented to the Cardinal the precious piece of paper which Athos had forced from milady, and which he had given to D'Artagnan, to serve him as a safeguard.

His eminence took the paper, and read in a slow voice, dwelling upon every syllable:

> It is by my orders that the bearer of this paper has done what he has just done.
>> At the camp of Rochelle, this fifth of August, 1628.
>>> Richelieu

The Cardinal, after having read these two lines sank into a profound reverie; but he did not return the paper to D'Artagnan.

"He is meditating what sort of punishment he shall put me to death by," said D'Artagnan to himself, "Let him; ma foi! he shall see how a gentleman can die!"

The young musketeer was then in an excellent disposition to suffer heroically.

Richelieu still continued thinking, twisting and untwisting the paper in his hands.

"I am lost," said D'Artagnan to himself.

And he bowed profoundly before the Cardinal, like a man who says, "Lord, thy will be done!"

The Cardinal went up to the table, and, without sitting down, wrote a few lines upon a parchment of which two-thirds were already filled up, and affixed his seal to it.

"That is my condemnation," thought D'Artagnan; "he will spare me the ennui of the Bastille, or the tediousness of a trial. That's very kind of him."

"Here, monsieur," said the Cardinal to the young man, "I have taken from you one signed blank to give you another. The name is wanting in this commission; you can write it yourself."

D'Artagnan took the paper hesitatingly, and cast his eyes over it; it was a lieutenant's commission in the musketeers.

D'Artagnan fell at the feet of the cardinal.

"Monseigneur," said he, "my life is yours—henceforward dispose of it. But this favour which you bestow upon me I do not merit; I have three friends who are more meritorious and more worthy—"

"You are a brave youth, D'Artagnan," interrupted the Cardinal, tapping him familiarly on the shoulder, charmed at having subdued the rebellious nature. "Do with this commission what you will; only remember that though the name be a blank, it was to you that I gave it!"

"I shall never forget it," replied D'Artagnan; "your eminence may be certain of that."

The Cardinal turned round, and said in a loud voice: "Rochefort!"

The chevalier, who no doubt was near the door, entered immediately.

"Rochefort," said the cardinal, "you see M. D'Artagnan—I receive him among the number of my friends; embrace then, and be prudent, if you have any wish to preserve your heads."

Rochefort and D'Artagnan saluted coolly; but the Cardinal was there observing them with his vigilant eye.

They left the chamber at the same time.

"We shall meet again, shall we not, monsieur?"

"When you please," said D'Artagnan.

"An opportunity will offer itself," replied Rochefort.

"What's that?" said the Cardinal, opening the door.

The two men smiled at each other, shook hands, and bowed to his eminence.

"We were beginning to grow impatient," said Athos, still waiting with Porthos and Aramis outside.

"Well, here I am, my friends," replied D'Artagnan, "not only free, but in favour."

"Tell us all about it."

"This evening."

Accordingly, that same evening, D'Artagnan repaired to the quarters of Athos, whom he found in a fair way of emptying a bottle of Spanish wine, an occupation which he religiously went through every night.

He related all that had taken place between the Cardinal and himself, and, drawing the commission from his pocket,

"Here, my dear Athos," said he, "this belongs to you naturally."

Athos smiled with one of his sweet and expressive smiles.

"My friend," said he, "for Athos this is too much, for the Count de la Fère it is too little; keep the commission—it is yours; alas! you have purchased it dearly enough."

D'Artagnan left Athos' chamber, and went to that of Porthos.

He found him clothed in a magnificent dress covered with splendid embroidery, admiring himself before a glass.

"Ah, ah! is that you, friend D'Artagnan?" exclaimed he; "how do you think these garments fit me, eh?"

"Wonderfully well," said D'Artagnan; "but I am come to offer you a dress which will become you still better."

"What's that?" asked Porthos.

"That of a lieutenant of musketeers."

D'Artagnan related to Porthos the substance of his interview with the Cardinal, and, taking the commission from his pocket,

"Here, my friend," said he, "write your name upon it, and become my officer."

Porthos cast his eyes over the commission, and returned it to D'Artagnan, to the great astonishment of the young man.

"Yes," said he, "yes, that would flatter me very much, but I should not have time enough to enjoy the distinction. During our expedition to Bethune the husband of my duchess died, so that, my dear friend, the coffer of the defunct holding out its arms to me, I shall marry the widow; look here, I at this moment was trying on my wedding suit. No, keep the lieutenancy, my dear fellow, keep it."

And he returned the commission to D'Artagnan.

The young man then entered the apartment of Aramis.

He found him kneeling before a prie-Dieu, with his head leaning over an open book of prayer.

He described to him his interview with the Cardinal, and, for the third time drawing his commission from his pocket.

"You, our friend, our intelligence, our invisible protector," said he, "accept this commission; you have merited it more than any of us by your wisdom and your counsels, always followed by such happy results."

"Alas! my dear friend," said Aramis, "our late adventures have disgusted me with life and with the sword; this time my determination is irrevocably taken; after the siege I shall enter the house of the Lazarists. Keep the commission, D'Artagnan—the profession of arms suits you; you will be a brave and adventurous captain."

D'Artagnan, his eyes moist with gratitude, though beaming with joy, went back to Athos, whom he found still at table, contemplating the charms of his last glass of Malaga by the light of his lamp.

"Well," said he, "and they likewise have refused me!"

"That, my dear friend, is because nobody is more worthy than yourself."

And he took a pen, wrote the name of D'Artagnan on the commission, and returned it to him.

"I shall then no longer have friends," said the young man; "alas! nothing but bitter recollections."

And he let his head sink upon his hands, while two large tears rolled down his cheeks.

"You are young," replied Athos, "and your bitter recollections have time to be changed into sweet remembrances."

𝒪

SIGNET CLASSICS from Around the World

☐ **THE OCTOPUS by Frank Norris.** The story of a titanic struggle between California farmers and a railroad which threatens to monopolize them. Afterword by Oscar Cargill.
(#CE1037—$1.75)

☐ **GULLIVER'S TRAVELS by Jonathan Swift.** The four classic voyages of Gulliver, which make both a fascinating fairy tale and a bitter satire. With 30 illustrations by Charles Brock and 5 maps. Foreword by Marcus Cunliffe.
(#CY1024—$1.25)

☐ **THE OX-BOW INCIDENT by Walter Van Tilburg Clark.** A relentlessly honest novel of violence and quick justice in the Old West. Afterword by Walter Prescott Webb.
(#CW1007—$1.50)

☐ **THE DEERSLAYER by James Fenimore Cooper.** The most romantic of Cooper's five "leatherstocking" tales of the American frontier. Afterword by Allan Nevins.
(#CE996—$1.75)

☐ **THE LAST OF THE MOHICANS by James Fenimore Cooper.** The classic portrait of frontier life. Afterword by James Franklin Beard. (#CW1054—$1.50)

☐ **THE CALL OF THE WILD and Selected Stories by Jack London.** The American author's vivid picture of the wild life of a dog and man in the Alaska gold fields. Foreword by Franklin Walker. (#CY1074—$1.25)

☐ **A CONNECTICUT YANKEE IN KING ARTHUR'S COURT by Mark Twain.** A modern American finds himself among the knights of the Round Table in this biting satire on medieval superstitions. Afterword by Edmund Reiss.
(#CY1073—$1.25)

☐ **THE AMERICAN by Henry James.** James's story of a wealthy, capable, candid American businessman who comes to France to select a wife from the ranks of the aristocracy. Afterword by Leon Edel. (#CE1053—$1.75)

THE NEW AMERICAN LIBRARY, INC.,
P.O. Box 999, Bergenfield, New Jersey 07621

Please send me the SIGNET CLASSIC BOOKS I have checked above. I am enclosing $_____(check or money order—no currency or C.O.D.'s). Please include the list price plus 35¢ a copy to cover handling and mailing costs. (Prices and numbers are subject to change without notice.)

Name_____

Address_____

City_____State_____Zip Code_____
Allow at least 4 weeks for delivery

More SIGNET CLASSICS You'll Enjoy

☐ **A SENTIMENTAL EDUCATION by Gustave Flaubert.**
Translated by Perdita Burlingame and with an Afterword by F. W. Dupee. Amid the Revolution of 1848, this is the story of a young man's love for an older woman.
(#CW579—$1.50)

☐ **MOLL FLANDERS by Daniel Defoe.** Afterword by Kenneth Rexroth. This lusty portrait of an extraordinary prostitute in 18th-century England added a fresh dimension of realism to the art of the novel.
(#CY1025—$1.25)

☐ **TOM JONES by Henry Fielding.** This long, richly plotted novel about the fortunes of Tom Jones, marked a giant step toward the achievement of realism in the novel with its first appearance in 1749. Afterword by Frank Kermode.
(#CE1021—$1.75)

☐ **THE ADVENTURES OF TOM SAWYER by Mark Twain.** The classic story of growing up on the Mississippi River is part of America's enduring heritage. Afterword by George P. Elliott.
(#CQ978—95¢)

☐ **THE MYSTERIOUS STRANGER and Other Stories by Mark Twain.** Witty, satiric stories by America's greatest humorist of the nineteenth century. Foreword by Edmund Reiss.
(#CY937—$1.25)

☐ **ROBINSON CRUSOE by Daniel Defoe.** The timeless story of a young merchant seaman's struggle for survival when he is marooned on an uninhabited island. Afterword by Harvey Swados.
(#CW1052—$1.50)

Have You Read these Bestsellers from SIGNET?

☐ **BRING ME A UNICORN: The Diaries and Letters of Anne Morrow Lindbergh (1922–1928) by Anne Morrow Lindbergh.** Imagine being loved by the most worshipped hero on Earth. This nationally acclaimed bestseller is the chronicle of just such a love. The hero was Charles Lindbergh; the woman he loved was Anne Morrow Lindbergh; and the story of their love was one of the greatest romances of any time. "Extraordinary . . . brings to intense life every moment as she lived it."—**New York Times Book Review** (#W5352—$1.50)

☐ **HOUR OF GOLD, HOUR OF LEAD by Anne Morrow Lindbergh.** The Lindberghs were the golden couple in a fairytale romance. And when their first child was born, the world rejoiced. Eighteen months later, tragedy struck . . . "A totally expressive, often unbearable record of an extreme personal anguish that followed the greatest possible happiness. Mrs. Lindbergh as a great gift for communicating directly her joy and pain."—**The New York Times Book Review** (#E5825—$1.75)

☐ **ELEANOR AND FRANKLIN by Joseph P. Lash. Foreword by Arthur M. Schlesinger, Jr.** A number 1 bestseller and winner of the Pulitzer Prize and the National Book Award, this is the intimate chronicle of Eleanor Roosevelt and her marriage to Franklin D. Roosevelt, with its painful secrets and public triumphs. "An exceptionally candid, exhaustive . . . heartrending book."—**The New Yorker** (#E7419—$2.50)

☐ **ELEANOR: THE YEARS ALONE by Joseph P. Lash. Foreword by Franklin D. Roosevelt, Jr.** Complete with 16 pages of photographs, this is the bestselling companion volume to the prize-winning **Eleanor and Franklin**. "Everyone who read **Eleanor and Franklin** will want to know the end of the story." —**Life.** "The story Eleanor thought was over when her husband died. . . . It is her capacity for love which shines through these pages."—**Los Angeles Times** (#J5627—$1.95)